DANGER AT SANDPIPER BAY

A RILEY HARPER MYSTERY

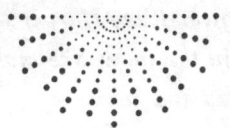

TRACI HALL
PATRICE WILTON

DANGER AT SANDPIPER BAY

A RILEY HARPER MYSTERY

by

TRACI HALL and PATRICE WILTON

A nor'easter off the coast of Maine leaves everyone stranded on Sandpiper Bay and Officer Riley Harper's courage is tested when she finds a dead body in the snow. She must find the killer before he escapes both the island and justice.

Officer Riley Harper faces danger of an unusual kind in Sandpiper Bay. A nor'easter off the coast of Maine is set to slam into their little island, cutting off all communication and putting the residents at risk. During the storm a killer strikes. Stranded, Riley and her partner race the clock to track the villain before the thaw, and possible escape.

PRAISE FOR "SALEM B&B COZY MYSTERY SERIES"

Mrs. Morris and the Ghost

"Once I started reading, I couldn't put it down! I'm psyched that I discovered this book just in time for the next one. Highly entertaining, incredibly fun read!"

"This mystery has everything—fun, love, heartache and suspense! I enjoyed reading and trying to help solve the mystery right along with Mrs. Morris! Can't wait to read another ghost story in this series!"

"I loved this book from the very first page. It was entertaining, the characters were enjoyable, there were surprises along the way and it is written so well."

"Compelling characters to a well-plotted mystery create an engaging read."

Mrs. Morris and the Witch

"The mystery was well-crafted, with plenty of suspense and red herrings to keep me guessing. I highly recommend this one."

"I loved this book. I mean, absolutely loved this book. The Salem B & B Mystery series is fast tracking it's way to my favorite cozy series of all time. It was a fabulous read and I can't wait to see what happens next!"

"How absolutely entertaining! Charlene Morris owns a B&B in Salem and has her own resident ghost. These books are exceptionally well written with fabulous characters. Upon reading these books I feel like I am in Salem visiting all the sights described within. I hope there are many, many more books to come in this series. Highly recommended!!"

Mrs. Morris and the Ghost of Christmas Past

"This is one of the most entertaining series I've read! Extremely well written with great characterization. If you want to leave "real life" behind pick up this book and laugh or gasp or cry or just enjoy the read. Enjoy!"

"This series is just plain awesome!! I love the characters! I love the setting! The B&B is a place I would love to visit and stay at. Just love it all!"

"The Salem B&B Mysteries is quickly becoming one of my favorite cozy mystery series. I enjoyed this third book immensely. The characters are engaging, the setting charming, and I was unable to solve the mystery, which is always a plus. The writing style flows effortlessly and the wintry Christmas atmosphere will leave you longing for the holiday season."

Great Series Starter

I absolutely loved this book. Riley Harper is such a great character in this book. I love the feel of the town she moves to. She proves that even though she is a woman officer, she is not one to mess with. Can't wait to see what is in store for Riley next.

After risking everything doing the right thing, Riley Harper packs up her Mum and her daughter and sets off to start over on an island off the coast of Maine. No good deed goes unpunished, and her pasts threatens to destroy her, despite the thousands of miles between then and now. There's a fine line between justice and loyalty...

Having accepted the only precinct willing to take her, Riley is now the newest addition to the Sandpiper Bay Police Department. Riley will have to prove herself worthy, or spend the next year in misery. Chief Barnes has let it be known that her being there wasn't at his recommendation...

For the most part, Sandpiper Bay is a community with a low crime rate, so the discovery of a dead girl, who was previously a "local," comes as a shock. Even more shocking, Lacey's death doesn't seem to be mourned by anyone on the island, except for the possibility of her best friend Chloe.

Initially, Chief Barnes seems certain that Lacey's death is suicide, but Riley feels differently. And, when the medical examiner agrees that the death is foul play, the chief designates Riley as lead investigator. With her past working against her, and everyone in town certain that "one of their own" couldn't possibly be the murders, Riley's investigation already has two strikes against it...

Who killed Lacey Killian? Was it an islander or an outsider? Can Riley figure it out, or did all the evidence and her future as an officer get washed out to sea?

Traci Hall & Patrice Wilton have given their readers a fantastic work of mystery/suspense/who dunnit. I look forward to more titles featuring Riley Harper and the rest of the Sandpiper Bay.

I absolutely loved this book. Riley Harper is such a great character in this book. I love the feel of the town she moves to. She proves that even though she is a woman officer, she is not one to mess with. Can't wait to see what is in store for Riley next.

Edited by Editing by Kimberly Dawn

Cover design by Mae from Baby Fresh Designs

Formatted by Bent Elbow Press

CHAPTER ONE

WIND BUFFETED THE FIAT LIKE A CAT BATTING A TOY MOUSE. Riley Harper, newest addition to the Sandpiper Bay police force, hunched over the wheel and dodged branches along the dark two-lane road from their rental toward the family's favorite restaurant, the Lobster Pot. Her mother, Susan, and her fourteen-year-old daughter, Kyra, chatted about Katie's birthday party—the only reason they were out on such a dreary January evening. Snow was in the forecast. Leaves and sleet danced on the pavement. Thick rain smacked the windshield.

"Was that a snowflake?" Kyra asked with excitement, nose pressed to the rear passenger window.

Riley really hoped not, though her daughter was thrilled about the long Martin Luther King weekend and *at last* being able to make a snowman. Sandpiper Bay had experienced an extremely mild winter, so everyone said.

This would be their first experience with snow. Her position on the east coast island had brought a lot of firsts. First time they'd seen an old man petting a chicken. First time she'd been given a pint-sized police car.

They reached the gravel parking lot and Riley breathed out a sigh of relief that they'd made it. Now her concern would be driving home before the snow fell. Another first? Driving in the white stuff.

"Here we are," Susan singsonged. Her mom, wrapped to her neck in a down coat, opened the passenger door and stepped out. The brisk temperature had definitely dropped in the five minutes since leaving home. The dash read thirty-five degrees when it had been in the forties all day.

"Kyra, honey, don't forget Katie's present." They'd bought the restaurant owner a gift certificate for a spa day in Bangor and tied it to a box of chocolates. Riley exited the car.

"Got it," her daughter said. Kyra, once out of the vehicle, clasped the box to her chest as a sly gust of wind almost stole it away. "Oops. That woulda sucked."

"But you caught it," Susan said. The forty years she'd worked with at-risk babies had given her an immense capacity for patience that Riley had relied on heavily in the last five months.

Riley led the way across the parking lot toward the front door of the Lobster Pot. Hundreds of sparkling lights in blue, red, and green decorated the outside in a festive reminder of the holidays.

Her mother swung open the front door. "What a fun Friday night."

The ladies had spent the long winter evenings with books, games, and movies. Riley no longer minded the forced relaxation. She ushered Kyra before her into the warmth.

"Sammy texted that she's going to the movies with Josh tonight." Kyra's tone held typical teenaged angst as her best friend in Phoenix had a boyfriend, and Kyra felt left behind. Riley wondered for the millionth time if she'd made a mistake by uprooting both her mother and her rebellious teen from their comfortable lives in Phoenix.

Riley brushed a strand of Kyra's long brown hair from her

face. Her daughter was pretty and smart, with full lips now in a pout. "You could invite a friend from school over."

"Nope. Waste of time. We are temporary." Kyra refused to make friends in Maine.

Riley was not above bribery in her parenting bag of tricks to bring a smile to Kyra's face and had been in talks with Sammy's mother to buy a ticket for Sammy to spend time over spring break, as a surprise. Once the ticket was bought, she'd tell Kyra.

A sharp breeze tickled her nape and Riley hustled inside, closing the door behind her. She unzipped her thick winter jacket. Coby Jenkins, handsome owner of the neighborhood pub, rounded the podium to greet them. He was thirtyish with sandy-blond hair and a flirty nature. "Hello, ladies." His cheeks dimpled as he flashed a smile. "May I help with your coats?"

"No, you may not!" Susan spoke emphatically. "But thanks." Her mom slipped off her jacket and hung it on a hook, along with her scarf. Kyra followed suit. Music and laughter filled the cozy interior, in contrast to the wintry chill outside. Lights twinkled on the inside windows overlooking the ocean, creating magical prisms. The shadow of a giant oak tree, large branches bare, was an eerie silhouette.

"Did Katie give you a job?" Riley teased. "You can add restaurant greeter to your bar owner resume. Who's running your place on a Friday night?"

"Valerie volunteered so that Kimber and I can be here for the party." Coby gestured to the dining area. "We saved you seats at our table."

"Thank you!" Riley peered into the crowded dining area. "Where's the birthday girl?"

"Katie's Queen Bee at the longest table there by the wall, with Matthew." Riley made out the ginger hair of her partner at the station. They'd forwarded the department phone to their mobiles since the chief was out of town, visiting his daughter and the triplets. The station closed at six, but an island cop was never really off duty.

Katie saw them and jumped up from her seat with a squeal. She hugged Kyra first, then Susan, and last, Riley. Bright-blue eyes twinkled in a round face and a tiara glittered from springy black curls. "You came!"

"Of course, we did!" Riley shifted the purse of her strap over her arm. "No way would we miss your special day."

"I'm *thirty*," Katie said in amazement. "Impossible to believe."

Carter, Katie's boyfriend, waved from the kitchen. His dark-brown hair was covered in a party hat rather than his customary chef's hat. "I hope you brought your appetites! Instead of a sit-down meal, our birthday girl wants thirty of her favorite tapas. I've been cooking all day." His grin showed that he was in his element.

Katie drew them past the podium to the dining area. Assorted tables had been set with plates and silverware in a rainbow of bright colors. Balloons and flowers covered every bare surface. A banner above the buffet read THREE DECADES OF GREAT.

"Happy birthday, Katie." Kyra touched the 'best friends' necklace identical to one Sammy had—gifts they'd exchanged before the move—and raised the candy box with her free hand. "Here's your present."

"Oh, you didn't have to!" Katie pointed to a round table stacked with gifts. "But I'm glad you did," she finished with a chuckle. "Go ahead and add it there. Sarah is getting drinks for everyone. Order whatever you like—it's on the house."

Another friend of Katie's entered the restaurant and Katie left Riley to greet her with a happy shout.

"We're over here," Susan said to Riley, smiling at Katie's enthusiasm.

Kyra peeled off to add their box to the pile and Riley followed her mother to the table. She kissed Maria's cheek and high-fived adorable six-year-old Dante. Kyra sometimes babysat him when Coby and Maria went out.

Between Coby and Kimber, Coby's full-time bartender, was an attractive man with dyed black hair and loads of tattoos. Susan settled on the corner between her and Wyatt Michaud. The ferry boat captain hopped up to push in Susan's chair. Was that a hint of pink on her mother's cheeks? "Hello," her mother said to the others.

Kimber raised a tumbler filled with red liquid and fruit. "Hi, Riley. Meet Tamara, my old college roommate. Tamara, this is Sandpiper Bay's first female police officer."

"Hi!" the sweet-faced brunette said.

Kimber put her hand on the guy's shoulder and squeezed before letting go. He winced. "This is Lars... He used to bartend at The Shack. He was before your time—lucky you."

Lars sipped from a long-neck bottle. "Don't be mean, Kimber. It's not sexy." The man saluted his beer to Riley. "I promise to be a good boy, Officer."

"Promises, promises." Riley laughed. "Nice to meet you." Riley attributed her success in her career to her eye for detail. Lars was not quite thirty, lanky-thin as if food wasn't his priority. His words were slurred. He had *L O V E* across his right hand, and the symbols of playing cards across his left—hearts, spades, diamonds, and clubs. He had a gold-filtered cigarette above his ear.

Kyra joined them and Riley didn't miss the way Lars's eyes brightened on her daughter. She cleared her throat with a warning glare. "My *daughter*, Kyra."

Lars took another drink and looked away. Smart man. Riley turned to Coby. "Lars used to bartend for you?"

"*Used* to," Coby said.

Kyra sat a little straighter after Lars's perusal. Kimber raised her sangria glass in a mocking salute to Lars. "Lars left us high and dry for a position in Bangor. Coby, why are you being so nice tonight? Please tell me you're not giving Lars his job back."

Coby's mouth flattened.

"Hey! Why not? I've turned over a new leaf." Lars grinned and the group all laughed at his hangdog expression. Kyra giggled and snuck glances at him. Trouble with a capital *T*. Riley hoped he wouldn't stick around.

"I sure hope so. The way the wind is blowing, the ferry won't be running tomorrow, so we can't send you back to the city," Captain Wyatt drawled. "You got the last ride in this morning."

"Not to worry, Cap, I ain't going back to that stupid job in Bangor." Lars drank again, then turned the empty upside down, waving to the waitress.

Annoyance crossed Coby's face, but he held back whatever comment he might have made when Maria caressed his hand. Kimber gave Lars a sour look, then jerked her gaze to Riley, then Tamara. Tension bubbled like expensive champagne.

"You're good friends with Katie?" Riley asked, trying to understand why Lars was at the party if *nobody* liked him, not just Kimber.

"We've met a few times," Lars said, shrugging, then he turned to Coby as if he'd just had a terrific idea. "Think she'd give me a job?"

Coby shook his head at Lars, anger in the jerky movements. "Don't even—we had a deal."

What deal?

"Ta-da!" Carter left the kitchen to deposit a huge platter of various appetizers on the buffet. Riley couldn't believe the array of food. "These are Katie's favorites. Help yourselves, my friends. And leave room for birthday cake. Our Katie's lemon chiffon."

Sarah arrived at their table with a bounce in her step. She acknowledged Lars's gesture with a nod and turned to Kyra, Susan, and Riley to get their drink order too. Riley, because of the rules of her contract, couldn't have a glass of wine with her meal so she chose hot tea with lemon. Her mother ordered the sangria while Kyra went with a peppermint hot chocolate. "Thank you, Sarah."

When Sarah left, Riley suggested to Kyra that they go up together to select their appetizers. "Want me to bring you a plate, Mom?"

Susan, chatting with Wyatt, nodded. "That'd be great."

Kyra led the way, and they stopped to speak with Matthew, who was digging into a tall plate of savory foods. Her daughter's eyes widened. "How are we supposed to choose?"

Riley studied the stacked buffet, determined to give it her best shot. "We'll take a little of each and save room for cake."

Kyra giggled at the decadence and went for it—she no longer avoided foods that were different and hardly ever complained about the lack of a Golden Arches on the island.

Riley loaded two plates and she and Kyra returned to the table. Coby and Lars were in heated discussion at the podium. Wyatt hurried to the buffet. Maria shared slices of prosciutto on a crostini and bites of snow crab with Dante.

"Thanks, hon," Susan said, making room before her for the feast.

"Welcome. What's up with Coby?" Riley asked as she sat.

Maria gestured for Riley to lean closer. "He's breaking the news that Lars needs to find another place to stay after tonight."

Hmm. "This was a surprise visit?" Riley asked.

Maria didn't crack a smile. "Coby said he showed up around two at The Shack, acting all humble and apologizing."

Kyra peeked over at the angry pair near the podium. Coby's face was flushed, and Lars had his arms wide, his voice loud. "They're arguing."

"They have a history, but Coby always wants to see the best in people." Maria popped a piece of crab between her lips. "The way Lars is acting tonight proves that a leopard doesn't change his spots, eh?"

Wyatt returned, and the conversation moved on to school and when Kyra might babysit Dante again. Riley ate some lobster bites, content to people-watch while she sipped her tea. She knew most of the guests, but not all.

At the far table, Matthew was telling jokes to someone she'd never met. Katie was shoulder to shoulder with him, and Riley guessed he was Katie's brother by the same blue eyes and black curly hair. Carter got up and darted to the kitchen. Lars and Coby paced the front of the restaurant, the conversation heated.

A blustery wind smacked against the plexiglass outside the windows, followed by a tree branch from the giant oak. Riley's heart thumped and Kyra sent her a frightened look.

Wyatt saw Kyra's reaction and raised his gin glass. "Don't worry, sweetheart. We've got a wicked storm comin' in late tonight. This is just the first gusts of the front."

"Really?" Susan's brow crinkled. "We thought it was only supposed to snow a foot or so."

"Ayuh. Maine's weather is temperamental," the captain said. "Like a beautiful woman." He tipped his glass toward Susan's sangria.

"Oh!" Her mom flushed.

Lars and Coby returned, both men wearing false smiles. Coby plunked down to finish his food while Lars grabbed his beer and went to the podium with his phone, making a few calls. The wind howled through the cracks of the old wooden building. Branches scraped the exterior window with a screech. Riley rubbed her arms. Thick sleet smacked the pane. Wyatt had said a *storm*. That was different than fluffy layers of white snow.

"Screw you," Lars said, slamming his phone against the podium. A pack of smokes fell from his back pocket, and he grabbed them fast, teetering. Seemed Lars didn't have a lot of friends in town.

Coby eyed the ceiling as if to ask the Almighty for a miracle.

Kimber leaned across the empty seat so she was nose to nose with Coby. "You kept your promise?"

"Yeah." Coby pushed his plate away. "He knows."

Kimber's lower lip jutted as she glanced at Lars, who sauntered back to the table. "Good. Tamara, remember what I told you about Emily earlier? Don't be charmed by Lars."

"I heard that," Lars said as he dropped into his chair. "You sound bitter, babe. There are plenty of fish in the sea."

"Oh!" Kimber turned her chair so that she faced Tamara.

A large pounding jackhammered against the window—next was a crack of glass. Captain Wyatt turned in alarm.

"That's some gust, Captain," Susan said dryly. "Time to be worried?"

"Nah," he said, finishing his gin and tonic. "We'll be fine. Nor'easters are common—we've had an unusually warm winter. Not that *you* would notice, being from Arizona. I'll help Carter tape the glass for reinforcement before we go home tonight." Wyatt patted Susan's hand. Her mom actually allowed it.

Just then, Carter brought out a large yellow cake with thirty candles from the kitchen and set it before Katie. "For you, beautiful. Happy birthday to you..."

The lights in the dining room flickered. Apprehension tickled Riley's back.

"Happy birthday, dear Katie," they all sang. "Happy birthday to you."

As they clapped and cheered, a crash reverberated through the roof, shaking the building. The lights went out and plunged the dining room into darkness.

Riley reached for Kyra, her gaze on the moonlight coming from the window just as the large oak branch broke through the pane, shattering glass everywhere.

CHAPTER TWO

RILEY SLIPPED HER ARM AROUND KYRA'S TREMBLING SHOULDERS, but her daughter kept her composure in the chaos of the broken window which allowed torrents of wind and sleet inside. The candles went out on Katie's birthday cake and the dining room was dimly lit by the few pillars on the tables protected in vases.

Dante cried and Maria snuggled her son close. Six was such an innocent age. Susan, always calm, reached for Riley and Kyra's hands before she turned to the ferry captain. "Well, Wyatt? Cause for concern yet?"

The captain smoothed his palm over his jaw, not hiding a smile. "No, ma'am. Probably a branch broke off and hit the roof. We need to board up the window and sweep up the glass, is all."

Coby jumped to his feet, pushing the chair back. "I'll get the broom since I know where it is. You ladies sit tight and be careful."

Riley didn't care for being delegated to the table and stood up to see where she could best lend a hand. Her mom also bristled but she stayed put and didn't argue.

Carter hurried past them to the foyer and beyond. "Lemme

flip the breaker and hope the power comes back on; if not, I'll fire up the generator."

Katie's eyes were giant blue discs in her pale face. She stood, staring at the broken window, her hand at her chest. "This is an epic birthday, complete with near heart attack. I can't believe that happened!"

Don, a very handsome man, Riley noted, chuckled and gave Katie a hug. "One for the books, sis. You and Carter were just talking about trimming that tree, weren't you?"

The lights flickered back on. Coby swept the glass away from the window while Carter and Don held plywood and Wyatt hammered the nails in, which blocked the window from the wind gusts and bad weather. Matthew gathered the glass into a metal trash can.

Maria passed Dante to Kyra. "Do you mind keeping him occupied? I'll head into the kitchen to put the food away."

Kyra sat next to Dante and smiled at him. "Okay. This is pretty exciting, huh?"

Dante's expression was more cautious than excited. Kyra distracted him with talking about *Paw Patrol*, his favorite cartoon.

Riley decided to clear the dishes and bring them to the kitchen. Kimber and Tamara also pitched in, as did her mom. Everyone was accounted for, except for Lars. Where the heck was he? Riley discovered him sprawled out on a bench away from the noise of productivity, his leather jacket wadded beneath his head as a pillow while he waited for Coby and lazily sipped on a beer.

"Thanks, everyone," Katie and Carter said after things were tidied and they'd gathered around the table. Each guest had been sent home with a thick slice of moist lemon chiffon cake. "I love our island community. Please take care now." Katie's gaze turned to Riley. "Especially you, since you've never been in the snow before."

"I'll drive slow as molasses in wintertime." Riley deeply appreciated the island vibe where folks watched out for one another.

Matthew snapped his coat and stacked two containers of cake. "Want me to follow you home, Riley? Your car might not handle the weather so great."

Even though it was her fear too, Riley immediately shook her head. "No, thanks!"

"All righty then. See you in the morning, Harper. Bye, every-one!" Matthew raised his free hand and hurried out.

Coby helped Maria into her jacket. Kimber and Tamara had already gone home. "Call when you get to your place," Coby told Maria. "Lars and I won't be too much longer after you. Come on, already, dude." He scowled at Lars.

If Lars hadn't shown up out of the blue wanting his job back, Coby would probably be staying with Maria—that might account for the irritated looks he kept giving Lars, who rubbed bleary, bloodshot eyes with the knuckles on his *L O V E* hand. "See ya," he told Dante with a smirk. "Don't wanna be ya."

"We'll be fine." Maria tugged Dante toward her, her upper lip curled at Lars before she turned to Coby. "Good luck." The mom and son left, shoulders braced against the night as they rounded the podium, out of sight.

Each time the door opened, cold snuck into the restaurant, along with frosty rain. They said their goodbyes to Katie, Carter, and Don and headed toward the foyer.

Kyra zipped up, wrapping her scarf around her neck. Riley snugged into her coat and palmed her car keys. Wyatt helped Susan, and her mom didn't protest as the captain offered her jacket to her.

Wyatt clamped his hand on Riley's shoulder. "If there's one thing I've learned about you, Officer, it's that you stay cool in harsh situations. You'll get through this fine."

Susan nodded confidently and Kyra, a little doubtfully, but they opened the door and went outside. Riley blinked at the snowy sleet sticking to her lashes. Thick and white. Frosty. *Snow.*

The parking lot lamp was on and they were one of three cars left. Wind howled menacingly. Riley unlocked the doors to the Fiat with the fob and they all climbed in.

"You're okay?" Susan murmured as Riley gripped the wheel. Her mom set the bag of cake slices at her feet.

"Yep." Riley started the car and smiled, determined to put on a brave face. "Well, that is one birthday party that we'll never forget. Did you both have a good time?"

"Yeah. I sent Sammy a video of the window and she can't believe it. Wait until she sees the snow!" Her daughter's voice quivered with excitement.

Riley left the gravel lot and drove onto the two-lane paved road toward the house. Wind rocked the Fiat back and forth. "Dante just keeps getting cuter by the minute." She hoped that the weight of three people might hold the car steady. "What on earth is *Paw Patrol?*"

The pavement was slick from the wet snow, but Riley kept her foot calmly on the pedal, going around twenty miles an hour rather than thirty-five as was the posted speed limit. Neither passenger complained. It was like being inside a snow globe, with thick flakes sailing around them.

"You'd like it, Mom. All about keeping law and order. Maria asked if I'm free on Friday and I told her yeah. I've made enough from babysitting money to get that new jacket I want," Kyra said, speaking each thought as it came. "Can we please go to Portland? They have more shops to choose from."

Half-listening to her daughter's chatter, Riley slammed on the brakes as a deer darted across the street. Kyra squealed, and Susan braced her hand on the dashboard. Riley swallowed, her heart hammering in her chest. The car skidded but the tires found traction and they stopped in time. The deer pattered into the trees, safely out of sight.

"That was close," Kyra breathed out.

Her mom slowly released the dashboard and sat back, her face pale. "I thought it was just a shadow in the snow."

Riley continued with caution until they were a block from the dirt driveway leading down to their place, when the wind really picked up. Pine and oak trees swayed in gale force gusts. The main road was strewn with broken branches and debris. The Fiat bravely fought its way through like *The Little Engine That Could.*

This was much windier than Riley had assumed. Could the windows at the house break, like the one at the Lobster Pot? The picture windows were hopefully hurrican-proof, but there was so much glass! Apprehension had her gripping the wheel. Sweat gathered along her upper lip.

Riley rounded the last corner before their turn—a spindly pine had toppled and blocked the road. She instinctively pumped the brakes but this time the pavement was slick from the snow and the car spun like a top...coming to a halt just inches from the tree. Her mom grasped the passenger door handle and Kyra made a peep of fear.

Exhaling, Riley took stock of the situation—all three of them were fine. They hadn't hit the tree, but it was so long they were unable to go around on either side. The wipers frantically tried to keep up with the wet snow, but it was too much. All she could see was white. How could this whiteout happen so fast?

"We're going to need to walk down to the house, all right?"

Kyra didn't say anything, and neither did Susan.

Riley carefully drove the Fiat off the street and parked it on the side of the road closest to their house. Through the thick white blanket, she could just make out the blue paint on the trim.

"Mom, I don't like this," Kyra announced. As if Riley had control over the weather.

"Me either." Riley unsnapped her seat belt and turned to face them. "We have two choices. We camp in the car overnight, or we hold on to each other and make our way toward the house. It's visible and not far. I know we can make it—we might get wet, but it beats staying here."

Susan locked eyes with her. "I agree. Let's make a run for it."

Kyra sniffed back courageous tears. "Lead the way, Mom."

Susan got out first, holding the cake in one hand and offering the other to Kyra to help her out of the back. Riley grabbed her purse and keys, then joined them outside, locking the Fiat. It already had snow collected on the top. The three walked arm in arm down the driveway that had an inch of white covering the dirt. Kyra giggled nervously after her heel caught on a stick and she slipped.

"This is quite an adventure," Susan said once they were on the way again.

That was one way to view the situation, Riley thought.

The forest of trees helped protect them from the force of the winds. They reached the door at last. She glanced back and could barely see the Fiat through the flurries.

With shaky fingers, Riley was able to get the key in and turn the lock. They went inside, then looked at each other and laughed with relief.

"Home! Safe and sound," Riley said, flicking on the light switch. She said a prayer of gratitude for that fact. A deer, a tree…was she being tested?

"I'm impressed," Susan said as she hung up her down jacket.

Riley toed off her shoes next to Kyra's, her adrenaline pumped. "Trial by fire!"

"Not fire, Mom, but snow! I can't *wait* to go sledding tomorrow." Kyra ran to the window to watch the snow fall as the magical flakes covered the rocks around the bay.

Now that she and her family were all safe inside, Riley had to admit that it was lovely.

"I think I might stay up with a cup of tea," Susan said, heading to the picture window next to Kyra. "Want one?"

"I do, Nana. It's so pretty."

Riley sighed as her mom and her daughter leaned next to each other. That sight was just as beautiful as the snowfall. "That sounds fun, but I need to hit the hay for tomorrow. Night!"

She climbed the stairs and readied for bed, remembering to send Matthew a text about the Fiat. She'd need a ride in the morning, and someone would have to move the tree. The spinning circle over the outgoing text message indicated it was searching for service. The internet wasn't connecting but did that circle thing as it searched. Ten minutes later, the message was sent and the phone dinged. Matthew replied with a thumbs-up emoji. At that, Riley slept soundly.

She woke in a panic after a bad dream where the little Fiat was caught in a tornado, like *The Wizard of Oz*, and it landed on Chief Barnes's house. Sitting up, she pushed back the covers.

The digital clock by her bed was blank so she reached for her cell phone—seven thirty. Matthew was to pick her up in twenty minutes. Riley went into the bathroom and realized that the power was off.

Crap. A cold shower later, she'd dressed and went downstairs. Her mom was at the counter with a glass of water.

"Morning, Mom." She gave Susan a peck on the cheek. "No power. I'll call the energy company when I get to the station. Hopefully it'll be back on soon."

"I'll get a fire started, and we have plenty of blankets. We'll be fine." Susan walked to the window overlooking the bay. "It's really beautiful."

Riley joined her, in awe of the foot or more of snow that had fallen and piled up outside. "It's like a scene out of *Frozen*, isn't it?"

"Gorgeous. And cold." They returned to the kitchen and her mom passed a banana to Riley. "You should eat a little something. I might try to warm a pan of water on the fire for coffee." Susan grinned. "My preferred version of camping, with four walls."

"You can skewer croissants on the marshmallow sticks," Riley suggested. She noted the time and groaned. "I have to meet Matthew. Cell service is really spotty right now."

"He knows about the tree in the road?"

"I texted him last night. Listen, we have a radio system we can use to communicate if the cell phones aren't working. When the chief told me about them, I had no idea they'd come in handy." She felt guilty leaving her family in the cold while she went to work.

"I'll figure out the radio, Mom." Kyra rubbed her knuckles over sleepy eyes. The action reminded her of Lars. She hoped he hadn't given Coby any trouble.

"Thanks. I'll check in with you later and try to come home for lunch. Have a really great day, okay? Enjoy the snow!"

Kyra hugged Riley, then grabbed a napkin and two big croissants, heading to the living room where Susan was starting the fire. "Bye, Mom!"

Riley bundled up and trudged her way along the incline to the road. Her leg sunk into the fresh snow, making each step a workout. The birds chirped and squirrels chattered, as if to share the joy of the first snow.

When she reached the Fiat, Matthew was waiting for her, the police car running. He dragged one end of the skinny tree to clear the street. Riley helped him and noticed that the Fiat had a flat and a broken windshield. "When did that happen?"

Matthew kicked the good tire. "Bad night, huh?"

"A little different from our Phoenix weather—we had no power this morning, but Mom's got a fire going."

"Climb in and get warm. I'll radio Nelson Bach, the tow truck driver, to bring your baby to the auto shop. As for the rental, well, the power should be back on anytime. Totally normal after a heavy snow."

Riley wrenched the door open, and it creaked in the cold. None of this was normal. "How do people get around during the winter? Snowmobiles?"

"Some. Others do it the old-fashioned way and use cross-country skis. That's why the chief and I have snow tires and chains."

She made a face. "Thanks for rubbing it in." It was hard not to be a tiny bit jealous.

Riley trailed her gloved hand over the cream-colored leather interior, while Matthew swept the fresh snow off the windshield. When it was cleared, he waved at her, smiling broadly. Freckles dotted his cheeks, and she was reminded of Opie from *The Andy Griffith Show*.

Matthew shed his gloves and tossed them into the back seat while Riley admired the GPS system, the deluxe Sirius channel, and his standard radio. He turned the car around and drove toward Main Street.

Chief Barnes wouldn't spend an extra penny to keep her here. Not yet. One day he'd see her worth and beg her to stay. Would she? That was the question. Kyra refused to even make temporary friends.

Her outstanding fifteen-year career had been broadsided when her eager new partner decided to play hero by drawing his weapon and shooting a man with his hands in the air. Nobody had wanted the truth and they'd dragged her through the mud when she'd spoken it.

Matthew tilted his head to the dash, one hand casually on the wheel. "So, what's your pleasure? Ma bought me a year's subscription to Sirius, but I've only listened to country, unless I'm driving my nieces around. They like the Disney channel."

"Classic rock?"

They listened to Billy Joel's "We Didn't Start the Fire" and it amazed her that Matthew knew all the words—he pretended his fist was a microphone as he belted out the lyrics.

The police radio made a crackling noise. Matthew clicked it on as Riley shut Billy off. "Officer Sniders."

"Hey, Matthew. It's Coby. I've called the station a couple of times but nobody's answering. Running late?"

Coby sounded uncharacteristically grouchy, Riley thought. Must have something to do with his unwanted guest.

"Chill out, my man." Matthew had one hand on the wheel and the other on the radio. "Riley's car got stuck so I was picking her up for work."

Coby cursed. "Listen, I have a problem."

Riley grabbed the mike from Matthew as the car swerved slightly on the eight inches of snow. "What is it, Coby?"

Matthew gave her a disapproving look—he also put both hands on the wheel.

She mouthed *sorry* but used her chin to point to the snowy conditions. He needed to pay attention, so she'd handle the radio. Her years of experience had to count for something. Yet, Matthew had lived here all his life, so that made them equal partners. He certainly had a better car.

"Lars vanished," Coby groused. "He *kifed* cash from my home safe and took off. I wanna press charges this time. I never should've let him stay at my place."

Riley had two questions—what the heck did *kife* mean, and what had happened between Coby and Lars before?

"Take it easy, Coby," Matthew said, gesturing with his chin for Riley to bring the radio closer to his mouth, so she did. "Ferries aren't running which means he can't have gone far. I bet the fishing rigs are safe in the dock too. You home?"

"Yeah."

Riley raised a brow at Matthew, who answered her unspoken question with a nod. Pressing down on the talk button, she said, "We can be there in a few minutes to take your report."

Matthew nodded. "We'll catch the rat for you." He turned the car toward Coby's address, back tires not sliding in the least.

"Will you brew coffee, Coby?" Riley asked, craving caffeine and wanting to avoid a headache. "We'll bring pastries."

"Consider it done." Coby ended the call.

"What does kife mean?" Maine had slang all its own and some of the terms were beyond her immediate comprehension.

Her partner snickered. "Ah—kife means Lars stole, that's all."

"Got it. Let's stop at Bake and Shake since it's next to the bar." Joan and Charlie Higgins's bakery was the best even off the island.

"No prob. I'll wait in the car if you want to run in."

Five minutes later, a pastry box was perched on the console, smelling sweet. She blinked against the glare of the sun striking the snow before it returned to its hiding place behind a cloud.

Coby was outside shoveling when they arrived at his house. He waved and rested the shovel against the porch. "Working off some of my temper. Sorry about that."

Riley smiled. Matthew clapped his friend on the back. Snow fell and she almost lost her balance but saved the pastry box at the last second.

They entered behind Coby through a foyer to the right and the open kitchen. The scent of fresh brewed coffee made her mouth water.

"Coffee smells good." Riley dropped the box on the small round dining table.

Coby offered them each a full mug. "Cream and sugar are on the counter—help yourself."

Matthew sat down and lifted the lid, choosing a chocolate

with sprinkles. Coby took a long sip of his black coffee while she added cream to hers.

"What happened last night?" Riley asked. "With Lars? Weren't you doing him a favor?"

"That bastard broke into my safe and stole cash. After I let him sleep on my couch. I'm an idiot for having him here. He claimed to be a changed man." Coby chose an éclair, scowling.

"Honesty is not the best policy for some people, you know. I learned that at police school." Riley smirked, picked out a cinnamon raisin donut, then placed it on her paper napkin after one delicious bite.

"Funny." Matthew finished his donut, sipped his coffee, then took out a paper tablet and a pen from his pocket. "What time did the theft occur?"

"Around midnight," Coby said. "We talked over a shot of whiskey when we got home from Katie's party... I just wanted to hit the sack and hoped another drink would make him pass out. Told him I didn't want him to ever show his face at The Shack, not to work or as a customer. Valerie, my other bartender, and Nate, my dishwasher, both know." He shifted from one foot to the next. "Kimber would kill me."

"How did Lars get into the safe? Did he know the combo?" Riley wadded up her napkin and reached for her cup. Coffee made everything better.

"He used my drill to break into it. I'd been in a deep sleep, but woke up to an awful grinding noise. It looks like he tried everything in my toolbox. Serves me right for getting a cheap one."

Riley leaned against the counter. Ballsy—and not very sneaky. Desperate. "Was there an altercation?"

Coby scoffed. "Like, did we fight? No, I chased him out the back door and into the snow. It was heavy and hard to see in the dark. The wind was crazy. I remember thinking he was going to freeze even with his boots and jacket. Not that I cared much. Obviously, he intended to rob me and sneak out while I slept, but couldn't get the damn thing open without the drill."

"What was in the safe?" Riley poised her stylus over the notes section of her phone.

"I don't know—cash. Passport. Birth certificate." Coby grimaced. "That moron. It's a nightmare to order that stuff again. I'm going to kick his ass when you find him."

"I overheard you say something about a deal last night—what did that mean?" Riley asked.

"I said I'd let him come to the party, on the condition that he'd behaved. He didn't. I caught him asking the waiter if he had anything stronger than alcohol. Last straw for me."

Matthew stood and raised his cell phone. "Let me get some pictures for our report."

"This way." Coby led them down a hall and opened a door to the right.

They entered an office that doubled as a second bedroom. The painting was on the bed, and the black door of the safe behind it hung by a hinge. Metal filings littered the carpet.

Matthew snapped photos inside the safe. "Nothing."

"Any idea of where Lars might have gone?" Riley scanned the room and the empty safe.

"His poker buddies might know." Coby smacked his fist into his open palm. "When you find him, I'd love to have a chat."

"Calm down," Matthew said. "Lars can't have gone far. He's gotta be hiding out nearby. We'll need the names of his friends."

"He didn't have any," Coby said. "None that were willing to take his sorry ass in, anyway."

Riley recalled the angry hang-ups last night at the Lobster Pot. "Coby. Kimber warned Tamara about Lars being a player and mentioned someone named Emily. Were Lars and Kimber an item?"

"No." Coby shook his head. "Lars wouldn't be at Kimber's;

trust me about that. As for his poker pals, Bernie Murphy might know better than me. I don't play cards."

"Okay. We can check at the marina." Riley made a note. "Where did Lars used to live while he worked for you?"

Coby gritted his teeth. "I think he rented a room at Tessa Barton's but I wasn't his babysitter for Christ's sake. It'll be on the W2 form at the office. I suggested Lars call her, but I guess he didn't leave the boarding house on a high note." He pocketed his hand. "Surprise, surprise."

Riley recalled Kimber's warning to her friend Tamara not to trust Lars. "Who is Emily? Kimber mentioned her last night."

Coby rubbed his hair. "Yeah, that's right. Emily Hamilton is eighteen and works at The Shack—not a lot of hours during the winter but Tuesday and Thursday for karaoke nights. They flirted, but I warned him to steer clear since he's twelve years older."

Riley jotted the name down on her phone. "Any other hearts broken when he left you high and dry? What about Valerie, the other bartender?"

"Nah. She's happily married and immune to Lars's line of crap." Coby waved his hand dismissively. "Everyone knew the score with Lars. Listen, Emily's a sweet girl who was taken in by Lars's attention. She doesn't flirt like that with the other customers."

Matthew finished taking pictures of the safe, the drill, and the tools. "Give it some thought and make a list of what's missing, all right? Drop it by the station later."

Coby blew out a breath. "Sure."

Riley walked back to the foyer, Coby behind her, and Matthew bringing up the rear. "If you think of any lovers or exes, let us know?"

"I will." Coby half smiled, calmer now that he'd reported the crime. Being vandalized was no joke, especially if you knew the guy. "Thanks for coming by so quick."

The officers put on their coats and hustled to the sedan. It was as if the clouds were feather pillows slit open to release downy flakes. Matthew drove them toward the main road. Riley asked, "Well, where to?"

"The station," Matthew said. "Let's get this report into the computer." He turned fast and the tires slid but then gained traction.

Riley leaned forward as they got behind a bright-green pickup truck with supersized wheels coming from the direction of Mackabee Woods. The rumble of big tires crunched, clearing the road ahead and piling snow along the sides that were normally ditches to handle water runoff.

"Is that a real snowplow?" She couldn't believe her eyes. It was orange and rusted in places, and eight feet wide.

"Yeah. Crash Moreno owns it. Dang it—we forgot to call Nelson about getting your car towed."

Riley looked at her cell phone and the fact that there were no bars. She tossed it to the dashboard in disgust. "Useless."

The windshield wipers flung snow back and forth. Here in town about three feet of snow had accumulated, but the drifts on the side of the road were higher as the plow cleared the street.

"Is that his real name? Crash?"

"I never asked," Matthew said. "He's a local dude who's been around forever. He operates the tugboat out of Murphy's Marina when the weather's decent."

Riley squinted, seeing two fuzzy forms in the cab. "Who's with him in the truck?"

Matthew burst out laughing. "His dog, Shazam. Man's best friend."

Laughing, Riley sat back. "Not much of a conversationalist though." Crash's truck turned right. Matthew followed.

She squinted at the snow piled high and focused on a pale

object. Somebody's dog or cat maybe? No fur, but skin tone. Her stomach clenched. "Stop!"

Matthew slammed on the brakes. "What?" The car slid around in a half circle and Riley gripped the dashboard—she hated being out of control.

Breathing hard, Matthew brought the vehicle to a halt, his cheeks flushed and his voice shaking. "This better be good, Harper."

She opened the door and raced to the pile of snow on the side of the road. A long pale forearm stuck up from the mound.

Matthew got out and slammed the door. "What's your problem? You realize yelling like that causes more danger…"

Riley checked for a pulse but there was nothing. She recognized the tattoo of *L O V E* across the knuckles.

"We found Lars."

Matthew's jaw dropped. He crossed the slippery white street and sank to his knees in the drift. "No, no, no."

The plow moved a little farther down the road, but it was snowing heavily and the green truck moved out of sight. "I'm afraid so."

CHAPTER THREE

RILEY SHIVERED AND HELD LARS'S STIFF FINGERS IN HER GLOVED hand. His *L O V E* tattoos were visible, which meant this was the right. His pointer finger was up, the rest curled into a fist. How long had she been in this position? She checked the time on her watch. Three minutes had passed since their grisly discovery.

She stayed in the drift even though her knees were numb, afraid to release the frozen hand until she was certain she could uncover the body. *If* there was a body. "We need to make sure this hand is attached to the rest of him."

Matthew grimaced and shot to his feet. He slid, and Riley steadied him by grabbing his calf with her free hand. Her life experience had prepared her for moments like this--she understood the world had dark places. He only knew this island and mostly good people.

She looked up at him and held his gaze. "You all right?"

His face was a touch green around the freckles, but he swallowed and nodded. "Should we dig him out?"

"Not yet. We need to investigate this scene and find out what happened."

"The plow dragged him here," Matthew said.

"We don't know that for sure. This ditch is a water runoff leading through the woods to the ocean. What if Lars's body was here already, and Crash just uncovered it? We can't assume anything."

"Gotcha," Matthew nodded.

Lars had left Coby's and darted out into the snowstorm. Coby had said Lars had on his leather jacket but that wasn't enough with temps in the thirties. Had he gotten lost somehow and frozen to death? How long would it take a body to freeze? It hadn't even been nine hours.

"I'll go get the markers and a shovel. Hang on." Matthew carefully made his way to the back of the police car and opened the trunk. The road had just been plowed so there were no tracks to follow, but there might be clues around the body and in the snowdrift. Riley shifted, her knees achy with cold. The clouds slowed to occasional flakes.

Matthew returned with the supplies to cordon off the area for investigation.

"How far are we from Coby's?" Riley reluctantly released Lars's finger. It stayed in the drift, and she relaxed. Lars was dead, and now it was up to her and Matthew to discover what happened to him.

Matthew dropped the supplies in a heap. "A mile maybe. Why?"

Riley envisioned how it might have played—the argument, Lars running scared at being caught stealing from his former boss, the only one to take him in. Coby had been pissed.

She leaned on the heels of her boots. "Could Lars have gotten lost and ended up here in the street? Hit by a car?"

Her partner nodded and gestured to the rows of houses. "Not all the yards have fences in this neighborhood. Lars could have cut across from Coby's no problem. It was coming down pretty hard."

Standing, Riley and Matthew made a circle of six feet

around the hand sticking up from the mound of snow. Flurries landed on her nose, and she eyed the gray sky with irritation that there was no on/off switch.

"The drift is what, four feet?" Riley did a quick visual of Matthew, who was just under six feet. It hit about his chest.

"Yeah." Matthew stomped his booted feet on the plowed street and knocked in the final stake with the head of the shovel. "Should we call the ambulance?"

"Yes, in a second. Chief too." Riley reached for the shovel. It helped her to balance on the awkward incline. She'd be careful to work from the outside of the circle toward the upraised finger. "I've seen some crazy things in my years on the force, but this might top them all."

Matthew's gaze remained on the hand. "Serge's on duty today. No chance Lars is alive?"

Riley shrugged. "No pulse, Matthew. I'm sorry." She just prayed it was attached to the rest of him. "Let's uncover him."

Matthew rubbed his clean-shaven jaw. "Why did he return to the island? After leaving The Shack the way he did, he shouldn't have expected a welcome."

"Not from Coby, anyway. Yet that's where he ended up." Riley gently moved snow away from the hand to reveal the wrist and then the forearm. More tattoos on his whitish-blue skin. An elbow. She would worry about *why* he had no friends later.

It was surreal, like excavating, and she had to keep the snow where it could be sifted through, if needed. "It's similar to sand, in a way. Only sand won't melt."

Matthew was contemplative as he watched her work.

Riley reached Lars's shoulder and exhaled with relief. She patiently kept at it until his torso and head were uncovered. He was facedown, his left hand beneath his body. "He's naked."

"Crazy and crazier." Matthew studied the figure. "Nothing's making sense here." Lars's dark hair was damp and icy to his scalp. "Coby would've mentioned Lars buzzing off in the buff."

"Coby said Lars had on a coat and boots. Also, there's no blood," Riley said. Her skin was chilled and now her heart was too.

Riley picked up the shovel and carefully flipped the body over.

Matthew cursed. Riley studied him closely until her stomach rolled and she tasted the donut from earlier at the back of her throat. Thick purple bruises curled around his neck and upper body, and he had a gash below his eye. Both were open and fixed.

Matthew brought the smart phone closer to Riley and the body. His voice shook but his hands were steady. When this was over, she would commend him for being steadfast and reacting quickly. Right now, her attention was on the victim.

Think calm. Professional. Detached. "We can rule out accidental death. Or getting lost in the storm or being hit by a car." Riley swallowed hard, and her belly settled. "He was beaten and strangled."

She ran her hand above the fingerprints.

"We need to call the chief." Riley set aside the shovel. It slipped and smacked into Lars's fist, the one that read *L O V E.*

"Want me to do it?" Matthew raised his phone.

"No, I can," she said. Barnes wouldn't be happy that a murder had happened on his island while he was away and she was used to taking the heat. "Is there cell service?" Her phone was on the dash of the police car where she'd tossed it.

Matthew shook his head. "We can radio."

"Okay." Riley knelt to retrieve the fallen shovel. Now that she was examining the closed fist from a different angle, she realized Lars was holding something. Adrenaline hummed. "Matthew, get the evidence bag and tweezers."

"Why?" Matthew gave her the requested items from various

pockets in his police uniform and she showed him how Lars gripped something, but they'd have to wait for his hand to unthaw before retrieving whatever Lars was holding. She scrambled backward and slipped down the drift.

"Let's see…" The left arm was at an odd angle. It was possible it had been broken. "Before or after death?"

"Huh?"

"The arm is bent awkwardly." Riley gently maneuvered the body to see the hand, but it was like moving a mannequin. Her pulse raced. "How long does it take a body to defrost?"

Matthew shrugged.

Riley stared at the body and the spotless drift of fresh snow. "Where is the blood?" His clothes and whatever he'd stolen from Coby, where were they? Surely, he had an overnight bag. Her cop brain wondered if Coby was perhaps using the call of a break-in to cover a worse crime—murder.

Matthew turned off the camera on the smart phone and switched it to audio so that he could record the conversation. "Lack of blood means that this happened somewhere else."

"Exactly." Riley stood, her teeth chattering. Her pants were soaked at the knee. "So, maybe Lars had been tossed in the ditch or maybe his body was caught in the plow."

"I'll get the route Crash used," Matthew said.

"Good. I'll call the ambulance to get the body to the medical center and then we'll break the unpleasant news to the chief."

She made the call, speaking to Serge Pearson, the senior paramedic on duty.

"Officer Harper," Serge said. "I was hoping for a quiet holiday weekend as it's just me and Trevor Dunfield on call."

"I hear you." She looked away from Lars. "You won't need the siren for this."

His teasing tone dropped when he said, "Dang it. Who?"

"Lars Sorenson. We need to get the body to the morgue. This

will be a criminal investigation, so I'll need you to take extra care with the deceased."

Serge gave a loud exhale. "Where are you?"

Riley gave him the exact street location. "In a snowbank."

"Hit and run?"

Thicker snowflakes began to fall. "You'll see. It wasn't accidental, that much we know."

While they waited, Riley tried to call Chief Barnes on the radio but there was no answer. Matthew used it next to get Riley's Fiat towed to the auto shop.

They both wanted to be busy rather than stare at Lars's frozen body and open eyes. The ambulance arrived seven minutes later, and Riley hurried out of the sedan. Matthew followed, slamming his driver's side door.

Serge was of medium stature with brown hair and a thick mustache. Trevor was short and broad across the chest. Both men seemed strong and had weathered, comforting faces.

"What do we have here?" Serge bellowed, glancing from Riley to Lars in the drift. Trevor opened the back of the emergency vehicle.

Riley pointed out the closed fist. "I'll need to have that open so we can see what's in his palm."

"Poor bastard," Serge said.

"You knew him well?" Riley asked.

"Just from the marina." He and Trevor wrestled the body on a gurney and at the last minute, Riley put one of the evidence bags around Lars's fist, just in case. "He'd hang out with us sometimes for drinks and fishing. A game of cards."

Trevor scowled at the snowbank. "I've been doing this twenty years and seen plenty of deaths, but not a murder like this." He slammed the back door of the ambulance after securing Lars's dead body inside.

Serge grunted. "Worst was when Old Man Hodgkins got caught and mangled in the whale hooks."

Riley held up her hand—she didn't need to add to the gruesome details in her mind. "Who's on call at the medical center?"

"Dr. Pru Lakshmi—she lost the coin toss." Trevor stepped toward the passenger side, walking backward. "Doc Rosenberg got to visit his family in Portland for the long weekend."

Riley hadn't met that particular doctor yet and she'd been hoping for Dr. Rosenberg. Oh, well—she couldn't call in a favor to a stranger. "Will you have her call me when we're able to see what Lars is holding?" She jerked her thumb to the ambulance.

"I'll relay the message." Serge stomped through the packed snow to the driver's side and got in, starting the engine. He poked his head out. "Stay safe, now. I hear there might be a real wicked storm brewing."

At the moment, the snow had actually stopped.

Trevor waved and hopped in the passenger side.

Matthew brushed snow off his hat. "We should get back to the station, file the report. We can try the chief again from there."

"What did Serge mean?" Riley got in the passenger side.

"Ignore him," Matthew said. "This is normal. Well, what's unusual is that it's been a slow start to the winter season. Serge just likes to cause drama."

"A dead body is plenty of drama, without adding bad weather." Riley sighed. Likely Chief Barnes would be livid to be stuck in Bangor with his family when he was needed on the island.

Matthew drove them toward the station. "I heard from Nelson about the car—he said he left the keys with your mom, and it should be ready to pick up on Tuesday, since Monday is a holiday."

"Thanks, Matthew. Appreciate that." She was feeling nervous about the uncertain forecast with a murderer on the loose. "I need to check on my family... It might be a late night."

"If there *is* a storm, are you set up with water and food? A generator? You haven't been through this drill before. Don't let

Serge freak you out. Things are fine. Last big blizzard I was eight, maybe, and I remember everything crystal and white. My folks tried to make a holiday of it for us and my sisters, but we knew something scary was underneath the laughter. You can't fool kids."

"They're smart." She peeled off her gloves and put her cold fingers near the heater in the car. "Who could do that to Lars, Matthew? He's got plenty of enemies but to leave him naked in the snow, well, it seems so heartless." She tilted her head back and closed her eyes. "Stupid question. We see the worst that people can do, more often than not."

"We'll find them. It's our job to keep folks safe. Nancy will come in, if we need her, and Rosita."

Nancy was the receptionist at the station and had welcomed Riley with open arms, unlike the chief. Rosita Sanchez was a support officer, which meant that she was the face of the department in the community but had no police training.

"Let's keep Lars's death to ourselves until we tell the chief and see what he wants to do," Riley said. "It would add fear to the situation when people need to stay calm."

"I agree with you. We'll radio him from the station."

Riley shook her phone that now had two whole bars. Should she try to call home while she had the chance? She dialed and it rang, but then the call dropped. She gritted her teeth. "This is going to make me crazy."

Matthew chuckled. "Should we drive by your place?"

Riley was tempted, but the report and telling the chief about Lars's murder was the priority. "We can, afterward. Do you mind making sure we have a generator, and that it's hooked up, just in case?"

"Happy to do it," Matthew said. His tone was sincere. "You think they're freaking out?"

"No. Mom is unbelievably calm and collected during emergencies. I try to be, and Kyra's been a champ during this move, even though she misses her friends." Riley looked at the snow which was thicker now. "Guess we can always store the food on the porch, if we don't regain power."

Matthew smiled at her and shut off the engine. "Way to find the positive."

Riley got out of the car and opened the door to the station for Matthew. The place was warm with the scent of brewed coffee wafting from the back. Matthew's smile widened to a grin.

They'd both been expecting an empty place. It wasn't the chief; he was in Bangor with his family, and it wasn't Nancy; her desk was clear. Which left Rosita.

Riley had grown to respect the woman, who was bright, energetic, and fabulous with the community. Everyone adored her.

"Hey, guys," Rosita called. "Come on back to the kitchen!"

Riley led the way down the hall. Matthew paused to toss his coat in his office, but she kept hers on, intent on java.

The ladies exchanged hellos and Rosita immediately got down mugs and small plates, nodding to a dish of blueberry muffins. "Perfect for a chilly morning. What did you think of your first snow?"

"The Fiat was a casualty last night, but we made it home. Almost hit a deer, and then a tree was down—but we're fine." Riley took off her jacket and found her phone. "Hope we are. I need to call home real quick and see if the power turned on." She wouldn't bring up Lars or his awful murder. Riley compartmentalized like any seasoned cop and knew how to smile through the crap.

Miracle of all miracles, she had cell signal and dialed the home phone. It rang...but nobody answered so she left a message. Hopefully all was well and they were out sledding.

"It's very common to lose power for hours," Rosita assured her. "You have a generator?"

"I don't know—Matthew's going to check it out later for us." Riley poured herself a cup from the pot and blew on the brew. The need to call the chief and find a killer and keep her family safe was like a sore tooth.

Matthew joined them and grabbed a mug. "Rosita, this is nice—thanks."

"You're welcome." Rosita lifted a brow. "I saw Serge and Trevor doing a drop-off at the med center on my way in. No lights, so deceased. Who was the poor soul? Heart attack? Stroke?"

"Lars Sorenson, actually," Riley said. Rosita was part of the team and needed to be brought up to speed. "Matthew, why don't you tell her about it while I call Chief Barnes? Before somebody else does."

Small island living meant gossip spread faster than fire on dry tinder.

"Lars? Hmm." A sad frown crossed her face. "I saw on the weather channel that we've got a possible nor'easter coming through," Rosita said. "It's why I came in. Not a big deal but we might want to keep an eye on it. The locals all know the drill. I've already put in a call to Wyatt."

Coffee in hand, Riley hurried to her office at the front of the station and flipped on the light in the room. Since moving here five months ago, she'd made it more her own with plants and pictures on the wall. A little personal but not too much.

The contract was only for a year, and it was doubtful that she'd extend it or that the chief would make an offer.

While Shelley Barnes might want her husband to retire, Riley wasn't sure that Bradley wanted it too. Besides, the idea of being trapped here during bad weather years on end wasn't something she or her family had agreed to, and her daughter came first no matter what.

Riley had taken this position to clear her name and restore her reputation—then they would return to the mainland, a big city and police department, but definitely not Phoenix. There were fifty states in this USA, and surely she could find something to suit her and Kyra, and Susan too.

The snow outside the window was thicker and dropping in clumps. She sat down and used the desk phone to dial Chief Barnes.

"Hello?"

"Chief! It's Riley."

"I knew it. Can't be gone a day without something going wrong." He covered the phone and murmured to someone, then came back. "What is it, Harper?"

She gritted her teeth and cleared her throat, determined to sound professional. "Sir, Lars Sorenson was found dead in a snowbank an hour ago. His body is at the med center."

"Uh-huh."

Riley knew she had his attention although he pretended to be bored. It annoyed her, and she was only human. "Naked, sir."

"Ex*cuse* me?"

She tapped her fingers on her desk. "Coby reported a robbery this morning, done by Lars. Coby chased him out around midnight—fully clothed at the time."

"What was he doing back in Sandpiper Bay? Lars was trouble."

"I guess he came over yesterday morning—Wyatt said on the last ferry running."

"Why?"

"I don't know—yet, sir. Last night he was drinking a lot, flirting with the women, then slurring his words. Kimber didn't like him."

She'd asked Coby if they'd had a relationship, and Coby had said no. She would need to talk to Kimber about Lars. The bartender was slender, but she had to have stamina and muscles to work behind the bar all night. It was Riley's job to suspect everyone.

"Yeah? Neither did Coby," Bradley drawled. "What else?"

"He was frozen, sir, and had something in his fist, but I couldn't examine it. Serge and Trevor let Dr. Lakshmi know that I needed to see what it was, asap. It looks like he was in a heated fight then strangled."

"I'm on my way," Barnes bellowed. "Can't believe I thought you two could manage things while I had a short holiday."

As if anybody could predict when a murder might happen! "We are fine, sir. Besides, Captain Wyatt said that the ferry isn't running for the next few days due to high winds."

He put the phone down and shouted for his wife. "Shelley, can you check if the ferry's going to Sandpiper Bay?"

"Dad," Riley heard a female say. "There's no ferry service. There's a nor'easter along the coast. You're stranded with us."

A nor'easter? There was that term again. Her chief picked up the phone. "You have to handle this, Harper. I'll call over to the med center and find out what's going on."

She didn't want to admit to him that she didn't know about the nor'easter thing. "All right. Cell phone has been intermittent, but we can set up the radios and stay in touch."

"Matthew told you about the last storm? I wasn't there, of course, but folks still talk about it. Ships on Main Street. Buildings snowed under. It was a disaster."

Matthew hadn't mentioned the details. Riley had the urgent need to touch base with her mom and daughter now that she'd informed Barnes about the murder.

"What's your plan?" Barnes asked.

She straightened in her chair and studied her Police Academy certificate hanging on the wall. It was a reminder that she'd earned her stripes even when she wasn't treated accordingly. "I'll start questioning folks who saw Lars yesterday. Lars stole from Coby last night around midnight. Coby caught him, and Lars escaped out the back door. He was found about a mile from Coby's place."

"Listen, Riley. You need to treat Coby like you would anybody. Right before Lars took off, what, five months ago, those two had a fistfight so bad that Lars had a broken nose. Lars could've pressed charges." Barnes drew in a slow breath. "Maybe he showed up on the island as payback. Question everything."

Riley opened her desk drawer and retrieved a pen and paper, jotting down *fistfight*. "We already asked Coby if there was a physical confrontation, and he said no, Chief. I'll ask again." And an overnight bag. "I'll also interview Kimber and Emily Hamilton."

"Why her? Hamiltons are a pillar in the community."

"She and Lars had a flirtation at The Shack."

He snorted. "Is that what folks are calling it these days? Keep me informed. And don't tell anyone that Lars is dead when you're questioning them, not with the ferry out of service. I'll call over to the doc and find out what's in Lars's hand."

She needed to borrow his SUV since her Fiat was in the shop. "Sir, I'd like to—" But Riley was talking to a dial tone.

Could this day get any worse?

CHAPTER FOUR

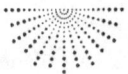

Grr. Had Chief Barnes hung up on her on purpose? Riley headed down the corridor to the breakroom, grabbing her coat and her empty mug. "Hey, guys?"

Rosita looked up from her coffee. Matthew slurped and set his cup down, alarm on his face.

"Yeah?" Matthew asked. "What's wrong?"

Riley glanced over at Rosita first, then Matthew. "What can we expect from a nor'easter? Forgive my ignorance, but I thought the winter storms were common and I wasn't to worry. What's changed since this morning?"

"We don't know if anything has," Rosita said in a soothing tone. "Weather is hard to predict. A storm can skip out to sea with a wobble or slam into the coast like a blizzard."

Riley exhaled and smoothed her jacket on the back of a chair. "That doesn't sound great. Blizzards."

"Think hurricane force winds combined with snow," Matthew explained.

Shivering, Riley asked, "When will we know?"

"Captain Wyatt has a weather sonar system and he's monitoring the situation. We just need to sit tight. Nine times out of ten, the storm fizzles out in the ocean." Matthew got up and patted Riley's arm. "Don't stress out. I can head over to your house and make sure that there's a generator and it's all set up. In the event we get more than a few feet of the white stuff."

"Thank you." For that, she wouldn't bug him about how he drove.

"Did you have another concern?" Rosita asked. The woman was a caretaker down to the tips of her toes.

"Yes." Riley had to take a chance and it was Barnes's own fault for hanging up too soon. "Do you know where Chief keeps his keys?"

They shared a look, and Rosita busied herself with dotting a few drops of cream on the tabletop with a soggy paper napkin.

"I tried to ask him if I could borrow it, but he was in a hurry to call the medical center."

Matthew cleared his throat. "Hang on. What are you thinking, Riley?"

"I'm *thinking* that I need a vehicle and Chief's is just sitting out back... Well, what he doesn't know won't hurt him, right?"

Rosita stirred her coffee with more vigor. "Mum's the word here."

Matthew wasn't as easy. "Why do you want to borrow Barnes's car? I can drive you if you need to go home and check on your family."

"We have a lot to do, Matthew. Especially if a storm does come. That means we have limited time to catch who killed Lars. What if they try to get off the island?"

Matthew sighed. "You have a point. What's your idea?"

"You go to my house and help my mom while I interview Emily Hamilton." Riley told Rosita, "She was a waitress with a crush on Lars, and maybe he tried to talk to her last night." She'd seen Lars try to call many people at the Lobster Pot with no positive results. Once they found his phone, they could trace his calls but until then, she had to do it the old-fashioned way and ask.

"She lives at home with her parents," Rosita said. "They're good people. Let me get the address for you."

Riley's shoulders dropped. Time ticked away. "Thank you."

"All right," Matthew said. "That's a smart use of time, but then we should reconvene here. Say an hour?"

"Sounds great," Riley agreed.

"I'll answer the phones," Rosita offered. "Folks can get squirrely when the weather changes."

Was squirrely a euphemism for murderous? "Thank you!" Riley zipped up her jacket and put on her gloves. "We've questioned Coby already, though Chief mentioned a previous altercation between Lars and Coby. We also need to need ask him if Lars had an overnight bag. Emily seems like the next logical choice. Oh, Rosita, can you get me Tessa Barton's phone number? I think Lars lived there before he moved."

"You got it." Rosita finished her coffee.

Matthew nodded his head to indicate Chief Barnes's office. "Keeps his keys on a hook next to the door. But don't say I told you or that I gave you permission. I don't want to get fired." He ran his hand over his ginger hair, causing it to stand on end.

Fired. She didn't see that happening. "I plan on telling him, and that it was my idea, the next time we talk. Besides, if anyone's going to get fired around here, it's *moi*."

Rosita stood and adjusted the uniform over her slightly plump midriff. She was proud of her curves. "The chief will be very impressed with you both if you catch the killer fast. Be careful though."

"I will, Rosita." Riley patted Matthew's shoulder. "Keep in touch, okay? Tell Mom and Kyra I'll see them later, but don't get them upset about the storm or the killer. Easy-peasy."

"They tend to skip along the coast, I swear!" Matthew raised his hand.

"It's all right. No need to curse." She chuckled. "Good luck."

"I've got it simple compared to you—the Hamiltons are salt of the earth types but if they don't want to talk to you, they won't."

Islanders were a different sort, Riley was coming to realize. "Should I wait for you?" She hated to waste time if the family refused to cooperate.

His lips curled in a half smile. "No, Riley. Go ahead. We need to find an extremely dangerous murderer, but I really don't think the killer will be at the Hamilton home."

Riley didn't care for his smug attitude. "Emily might have seen Lars last night or heard from him on the phone. She could point me in the right direction. You never know what clues will come from a conversation."

"Oh, I like that," Rosita said. "And you're totally right."

Riley picked up her thick coat. "We're all on the same page. Just a reminder, no mentioning that Lars is dead, until the chief okays it." Rosita and Matthew both nodded. "We'll meet back here within the hour."

Moments later she headed out the back door with the chief's keys in hand. There waited a newer model SUV with a set of brand-new snow tires. Obviously, the budget hadn't stretched far enough for her to warrant that piece of standard equipment.

Riley had the heater in the SUV running full blast when she called her mom.

Susan answered. "Hello!"

"Mom, it's Riley. Are you okay?"

"Of course, honey. The power came back on about an hour after you left and we've been outside. It's breathtaking. Literally." Her mom laughed.

That was great news. "Matthew will be there to see if we have a generator just in case we ever lose power again. You're having fun?"

"Kyra made a snow family that is absolutely adorable. She

and Sammy have been on video call all day. Right now, Sammy is the one that's jealous for a change."

Riley smiled and kept Lars's death to herself. "I can't wait to see them. Did she get the radio up and running?"

"She did. Not that I'm surprised—Kyra is a smart girl."

"Hey, try to corral all of the batteries. See if they match any lanterns in the garage. If not, call me if the phones work and I can pick some up while I'm out." There were a number of small service stations open as well as Murphy's Marina.

"Anything else?" her mother said dryly. "So far this snow has been amazing. I can't believe I've lived my whole life without it. I'm glad we're here together, Riley."

Her heart warmed, but the chill from how her mother would feel about a murderer on the loose doused any lingering satisfaction. "There is something else, but I can't tell you. Lock all the doors and windows. Watch out for strangers."

"What about you?" Susan quipped.

"Very funny. Keep an eye out for Matthew! Bye, Mom."

With the address to the Hamilton's home plugged into the GPS, which was global and not reliant on cell towers, Riley saw that she had an eight-minute trip. The road wound past Mackabee Woods. She didn't like the place but had no reason for the heebie-jeebies every time she passed by. She blamed Barnes and his scary stories. *Don't let your daughter go in the woods.*

Riley had a death grip on the wheel as she tentatively drove her boss's SUV through the still-falling snow. Drifts appeared out of nowhere, until after several heart-pounding minutes she reached the unpaved road leading to the Hamilton home. If this was the weather without a storm, she wanted the nor'easter to stay out to sea.

A black puppy the size of a pony raced around the yard in front of a two-story stone house with a covered porch. Green piney shrubs were on either side of a brown door. Tall trees surrounded the property. Houses in the neighborhood were on big lots, but too close to the woods for her taste.

Parking in the driveway next to a big truck, Riley turned off the engine and scanned the area. She carried a taser as well as her uniform police pistol, but in all her years, she'd never had to use it. For some odd reason she felt the trickle of apprehension slide up and down her spine when she got out of the SUV. The puppy scrambled over with a friendly body wag. His black fur was soft when she let him sniff her hand, and then she gave the dog a pat.

Taking a deep breath, she straightened her shoulders and walked with an outward confident stride toward the front porch and door.

She knocked. Waited. And with a little more force, she knocked again.

A male voice behind her said, "Can I help you?"

Riley hoped her flinch had not been noticeable. She spun around to see a young man, probably mid-teens, with a rifle loose in his hands. Unbuttoned camo jacket, jeans. Not a weapon, but an air rifle. If it had been real, and he'd wanted to shoot her, she would have been dead.

"I hope you're not planning on shooting me with that," she said calmly. "I'm Officer Harper. Is Emily at home?"

"Yup." He shifted the air rifle to over his shoulder and put out his hand. They shook; his skin was cold as if he'd been outside a while. "She's my sister; I'm Ryker. Why do you wanna talk to *her*?" He grinned. "What's she done?"

She had the feeling Ryker might like it just a little if his sister was in trouble. "Nothing. I have some questions Emily can help me with."

Ryker took his hunting cap off and ruffled his shaggy dark-brown hair. He opened the front door and went in, stomping his booted feet in the foyer. "She's the princess around here. I'm the trouble," he said, pounding his chest with his fist. The black puppy raced around his feet, tongue lolling with sheer dog joy.

She almost laughed. This kid was something else. "No, she's not in any trouble. Is there something I should arrest *you* for?"

"Hell no!" His cocky demeanor changed to accepting. "Dad always says I'm too smart for my britches, whatever that's supposed to mean."

Riley used the outdoor welcome mat to clear the slush from her boots. "There are worse things." She grinned and followed him inside. "Would you announce that I'm here?"

"Sure." He placed the air rifle by the door next to the closet and yelled, "Mom, Dad, we've got a cop at the door."

Nice.

The father appeared, tall and dark-haired like his son. A woman around Riley's own age with dark-blond hair piled on her head, clear complexion, hazel eyes, wearing skinny jeans and a plaid shirt, followed behind.

"Sam," the man said with his hand out to shake. "This is my wife, Lindsay."

The couple were both good-looking, which meant that Ryker had won in the genetics department. Probably Emily too.

"Officer Riley Harper." She shook their hands. "Sorry to disturb you but I'd like a word with your daughter, Emily."

"What's this about?" Sam asked. His jaw was set, his voice firm. Not angry, just protecting his own flesh and blood as a parent should. Not like her ex-husband Fraser who'd broken his daughter's arm in a drunken spree.

"A man that your daughter worked with at The Shack, Lars Sorenson, disappeared last night and I was wondering if Emily might have heard from him."

"Mom, Dad?" A pretty girl descended the stairs like teenaged royalty. Chin hiked, shoulders back. "I've got this." Emily was eighteen, which meant that Riley could talk to her without her parents, but since this was a preliminary interview, she didn't push. If it became necessary, things would be different.

"We'll stay for the questioning," Sam said decisively. "Let's talk in the kitchen."

Sighing, Emily gave up and just shrugged. Lindsay led the way. "I'll clear the dishes from the table so we can all sit and talk."

Emily helped her mom carry the soup bowls to rinse in the sink, then came back for the plate of leftover sandwiches. Her mother used a damp cloth to clean the table before they took their seats.

Ryker had shed his coat and stood with his arms crossed, leaning against the countertop. The puppy bounded between the dog bed and Ryker's boots, sniffing and wagging. "This is Bear," the teen said. "Mom calls him a mutt, but I think he's the best."

"We've all grown to love him," Lindsay said with an embarrassed laugh.

The home, smelling of fresh baking, was clean and attractively furnished. Not too fancy, but not cheap either. Framed watercolors decorated the hall. The kitchen overlooked the back forest and windows were floor to ceiling, making it seem like they were part of the outdoors.

Beautiful, unless you had a murderer hiding somewhere in those woods. Riley scanned the pine trees from her chair but saw nothing out of the ordinary.

Bear wrestled with a dish towel and brought it to Ryker to play with.

"Ryker, could you take Bear to your bedroom?" Sam spoke in a no-nonsense voice.

Without a word of argument, the teenager scooped the big pup in his arms. Ryker buried his nose in the dog's soft black coat, the dog's long legs dangling, and ran upstairs.

Sam brushed his hands and leaned back in his seat. "You mentioned that Lars was missing. We don't know where he is."

Riley noted a tick at Sam's jaw. "I'm hoping to discover a little about Lars's life in Sandpiper Bay." She gave the pretty girl a friendly smile. "Emily, you waitress at The Shack, correct? That's where you met Lars?"

"Yeah." Emily picked at her purple fingernail polish. "Lars bartended until about four months ago. I was earning a little spending money after I turned eighteen. Can't serve drinks until you are, you know."

"I do. It's nineteen in Phoenix," Riley said, keeping things casual.

Emily glanced up from her fingernails. "Oh, well, summer is busy but now it's not so I haven't been working as much. Karaoke nights are always a little wild. I still do Tuesdays and Thursdays."

"Sounds like a fun spot. I'm no good at karaoke however," Riley said invitingly. Conversationally.

Emily perked up. "My friends never miss it. They love to get on the mic and ham it up." Her expression turned guarded. "Lars flirted with everybody."

"Did he flirt with you?"

Emily blushed. Sam sputtered. "Em…"

Riley pressed on, wanting to keep Emily talking. "Did he ever discuss his close friends or mention family?"

"No. Sheesh, I hardly knew him. He was an acquaintance, nothing more." Emily turned her attention to her thumbs which were laden with thick silver rings.

"What about girlfriends?" Riley pressed. She needed to find out where Lars had gone after leaving Coby's.

Emily's mouth pursed. "He never told me who he was seeing. I didn't ask."

"Where is this line of questioning going?" Lindsay asked. She tucked a strand of blond hair behind her ear. Diamonds glittered at her lobes. "Besides, it's been less than twenty-four hours. Lars will show up eventually."

"Like a bad penny," Sam muttered.

Riley folded her hands on her lap, outwardly relaxed. Inside, she was very interested in this family dynamic. "It was extremely cold last night—he'd need shelter. We're looking for a friend that might give him a place to sleep."

"My daughter and Lars were co-workers." Sam's tone grew edgy, and Riley realized she might be pushing too hard. "Coby would know more, or that slutty bartender. What's her name, Em?'

Emily swallowed and glared at her dad. "Kimber? She's not a slut, Dad."

Kimber was next on Riley's interview list. "We will question everyone in order to locate him, in case he was caught outside in the storm."

"Have you checked the park?" Lindsay asked.

Emily slid her thumb ring round and round her thumb. Her face paled. Either she knew something about Lars, or she was also afraid of Mackabee Woods.

"We'll canvas the area when we can." Who could she get to do that, with just her and Matthew on staff? She hated to send Rosita out as the community patrol officer didn't have that kind of training.

"He's an adult," Sam said with a sneer. "If Lars wants to risk his life like an idiot, his choice."

Riley kept the theft of Coby's safe to herself, along with Lars's death. She smiled at each of the Hamiltons, eager to hear what they'd say next.

"I don't know why Coby would ever befriend him again." Lindsay's mouth puckered like she was tasting a tart lemon. "I heard Lars left the island on the sly, leaving Coby short-staffed."

"Mom!" Emily complained.

The source of the rumor? Riley shrugged. "I met Lars at the

Lobster Pot for a birthday party last night. He was there with Coby. My daughter Kyra, who is fourteen going on twenty, thought he was cute." She focused on Emily's reaction.

The teen bowed her head and blinked quickly.

"Good thing he went missing." Sam's eyes turned hard. "Lars'll probably be found sleeping it off in the woods or down at the shanties on the edge of the island with the other fishermen eking out an existence between poker hands." Sam glanced out the window. "Hope not too soon. I'd like to personally escort him out of Sandpiper Bay and drop him in the middle of the ocean."

Riley added Emily's folks to the list of people who despised Lars Sorenson.

"Dad. That's not very nice." Emily appealed to her mother, who glanced out the window toward the tree line.

"I think we're done here." Sam put his hand over his daughter's to stop her picking at her nails. "If Emily says she wasn't friendly with Lars and doesn't know where he's at, then what more is there to discuss? My daughter has never lied a day in her life."

Lindsay knocked over an empty cup as she rose from her chair. "Is there anything I can get you, Officer Harper, before you leave?"

Well, that was her cue to exit stage right. "No, thank you. I appreciate your talking with me. It's nice to meet you all."

Sam's jaw clenched.

Riley stood and put a hand on Emily's shoulder in passing. "You have nothing to worry about, Emily; we're just trying to piece together more information. It's a cop thing we do." She smiled at all of them. "Have a nice day. I'll see my way out."

She left the Hamilton home, noticing that the air rifle was gone. Snow fell in big fat flakes and the windshield of the SUV was covered.

Riley heard a movement in the bush about twenty yards

away and stopped with her hand on the driver's side door. "Is anyone there?" she asked.

More rustling. Could be an animal, even a squirrel or a bird searching for cover with the possible storm approaching. She'd heard animals knew before humans when danger was near.

"Ryker?" Her voice sounded a lot stronger than she felt.

She'd like to search the area but with all the open windows of the home, Riley would be easy to spot and her actions hard to explain. She got in the SUV and started up the slight hill, then pulled to the side. Her insides were telling her that she was being watched. Using the open door as cover, Riley surveyed the homes and trees. Most houses still had holiday lights and were festive though Christmas was over.

"Who's there?"

A raven flew out of the trees, squawking, large wings flapping. Her heart settled down as she realized it was just a bird.

Riley swallowed hard. Her nerves were rattled after the cryptic conversation at the Hamiltons; that was all. She got back into the SUV and drove past the woods to the main road, where she tried to call Matthew but there was no cell signal. *Don't mess with the woods.*

She used the radio and pressed the button, denying the goose bumps of alarm. "Sniders?"

"Whatcha got, Riley?" Matthew made smacking noises as if chewing gum.

"Nice family, as you said. Sam, her father, didn't want me questioning Emily more than I did and they politely asked me to leave. I think Lindsay knows more about Lars. Emily, too, but I'm not positive. I would love to get Emily aside." She tapped her fingers to the wheel. "That Ryker is a handful."

Matthew laughed. "I like him though. It's hard being a teenager on an island."

"You would know," she said with a wry chuckle. It made her feel worse for Kyra. "Any word from the chief?" Surely the doctor would call him right away. Because of how Lars's body had been treated, it was obvious an investigation was underway.

"Nope."

Riley swallowed a sigh of frustration. "What about Captain Wyatt?"

"He's still watching the monitor, but two other sources don't think it's going to hit. You never know with Maine weather—you prepare for the worst and hope for the best." Matthew popped a chewing gum bubble.

"I feel like we're wasting daylight with a killer on the loose." Her mind circled round and round. "How are things at my place?"

"The generator is all set up outside. It just needed gas. No matter what happens for the rest of the winter, you'll be ready. Wood's been stacked on the back porch for the fireplace. Batteries are stored in the garage. You have an extra can of gas too."

"Thanks. How's Kyra?"

He whistled. "We had a snow fight—your daughter's got quite an arm. She should play baseball."

"If she's interested, I'll sign her up." Riley scowled at the gray sky. Matthew was also good at compartmentalizing between life and tracking a killer. "It's a little dreary right now."

"Fair. You comin' back?"

"I don't know. There are so many questions I have. What about Kimber? And Tessa? Why didn't he go there last night?"

"Rosita has the phone number for the boarding house and the address." Matthew hesitated, then said, "You don't need me to remind you to be careful while poking around. His death might be personal, but what if it's not? What if we have a lunatic on the island?"

Riley had been trained to keep an open mind. "It might be revenge. It might be chance. The one *fact* we can take to the bank is that Lars's death was no accident."

CHAPTER FIVE

RILEY TURNED UP THE HEATER IN THE SUV, MOST OF HER brainpower on the crime, but a small part also noting the absolute beauty in a single flake of snow against the windshield. Gray clouds outside the vehicle provided a cozy cocoon.

In her yoga practice, she'd learned to be mindful and in the moment to alleviate high stress from a pressure-filled career. Often while meditating, answers rose to the surface. Watching the snow fall was peaceful. Matthew's words resonated.

"Matthew, is there a way for someone to *leave* the island? Winds were too dangerous for the big ferry, so surely a fishing vessel wouldn't risk it. Or am I wrong there?"

"Only the hard-core fishermen with sturdy boats made to withstand the battering waves." There was a pause, then her fellow police officer concluded, "I'll give Bernie Murphy a ring and ask if anybody's left his marina."

"That's a great place to start. Ask him about Lars's poker buddies while you're at it. Matthew, did you find the route the plow truck took this morning?" It was good they had pictures of the ditch because the snow had already covered their tracks.

She heard a chair creak as Matthew moved. "Yep. I've pulled it up for you to look at when you return to the station."

The snow was picking up speed as it landed on the windshield too fast to melt. "Sam Hamilton suggested that Lars could be sleeping it off in the woods or down at the shanties by the coast. You know anything about those?"

"We *know* he's not sleeping anything off," Matthew said, "but the fishing shacks might be a good lead."

"Fishing shack?"

"It's the most rustic excuse for four walls ever built," Matthew replied with a snort. "I'm surprised that so many have survived our extreme weather. Folks a hundred years ago would come over and fish off the rocks—most were guys, so no bathroom necessary, if ya know what I mean."

Riley arched a brow at the radio as she imagined a bunch of scruffy men out in the woods doing their thing… Camping without a flushing toilet was not her idea of a fun time. Like her mom, she preferred amenities.

"My granddad had one," Matthew continued. "We're talking a wooden pallet on the floor to separate your body from the ground, a hook for your gear, and a shelf. No sinks. Mom didn't shed a tear when it was broken apart a few years back in a summer squall. She thinks they should all be condemned."

So far, Riley was on Mrs. Snider's side though she hadn't seen one yet. She would keep an open mind. "Are they safe?"

"Hey now!" Matthew suddenly sounded protective rather than mocking. "Those sheds are a Sandpiper Bay legacy. Don't even think about ordering a safety inspection."

Riley puffed out a breath. "I've met the town council—they'd all turn a blind eye to a Sandpiper Bay 'heritage' site." The mayor, Ludwig Hoffman, was seventy years old and slick like a salesman. The other board members were all his cronies. If he had his way, Sandpiper Bay would *never* get a McDonald's.

"The council probably has looked the other way and possibly

a bribe was accepted once or twice," Matthew conceded. "Nelson Bach is the only one I know of who lives there year-round."

"He must have plumbing," Riley teased. Would Nelson know if Lars had stayed in one of the shacks?

"If you head down there, you can ask him." Matthew laughed, thinking he was funny, but Riley was already turning on the GPS. "Murphy's Marina has outdoor showers and fresh water outside," he continued. "It's very close to the shanties so maybe the guys go there to use the facilities."

Riley was reminded of the old days when people bathed once a week. Yuck. "Nelson is the man who towed my car?"

"Yep. He's a shrimper. During the harshest winter months there's not much for him to do so he'll help out where he can around the island."

The guy sounded scrappy and was probably strong enough to choke someone. "What do you think of him?"

"As in, could he have killed Lars?" Matthew burst out laughing. "Oh yeah. Go talk to him, Riley."

"What?" She hated not being in the know.

Matthew settled down and explained, "He's ninety pounds soaking wet. He can drink his weight in gin and considers himself a master at cards. I've had to bust up some loud arguments between Crash, Trevor, and Nelson."

Had Lars been part of that crew? "Why do they play, then?"

"What else is there to do on an island at night but drink and play cards? If you don't have a family, that is," Matthew amended. "Or a hobby."

She'd been plenty busy, but with a teenager in a new school, things were always going on. Riley thanked heaven every day for her mother. Susan Meyer was a much better parenting partner than her ex.

"What's Nelson's address? I'll go thank him in person, butter him up with donuts from the bakery, then ask about Lars and if

Lars used to hang out around the shacks." The bartender had to have some friends, right? And she knew Lars liked cards because he had the symbols across his knuckles.

Matthew blew a raspberry at her plan. "That won't get you far, Officer Harper. Bring gin from the liquor store. Rotgut's fine."

Her first reaction was to reject the suggestion, but she let it go. Riley would be invading Nelson's territory, so gin it was. "Thanks."

Matthew gave her Nelson's address. "Nelson's not particular," he repeated. "I doubt he even has taste buds left."

"And yet the island hires him to tow cars?"

"It's a freelance position. Before you argue, take it up with the mayor," Matthew said.

Not a battle she was willing to fight. She typed in the address to the GPS and switched on the windshield wipers. "It's really coming down," she said. "No way would my little Fiat handle well. What was the chief thinking?"

"That you wouldn't be here this long," Matthew answered in a gentle tone. "You've already proved him wrong ten times over, Harper. Unless you crash his SUV. Then you might be back at the starting line."

Riley turned the vehicle toward Murphy's Marina and the coast and ignored Matthew's laughter. "If you don't hear from me in an hour, come find me. You'll call Bernie?"

"Yep. Find out if any ships left last night or this morning. Good luck, Riley. And whatever you do, don't act all prissy, like a city girl."

She glared at the radio monitor. "I don't do that!"

He gave a chortle. "Over and out."

Having no cell signal, she wasn't able to call Kimber but she sent a text message to herself so she didn't forget. Tracking a criminal was all about following clues and threads that may or may not lead to the truth.

Riley maneuvered the SUV down Main Street, noting very little traffic. The residents were probably well used to winter weather and prepared to stay inside.

She reached the small liquor store next to a gas station that spelled BOOZE in flashing neon letters. Parking, Riley climbed out, careful not to slip on the snow, and went inside.

"Hello, Miguel." Miguel Garcia, the store owner, was in his sixties. His yellow teeth showed his addiction to nicotine, as did the smoldering butt in the ashtray on the counter. He saw her and moved it out of sight. All public buildings were supposed to be smoke-free.

Riley acted like she didn't see it. Liquor stores and robberies seemed to go hand in hand, so she'd been here quite a few times since her move.

"Hey, Officer Harper. Enjoying the snow?"

"I am." It was actually true. "Part of me wishes I was home with my daughter making snowmen, but maybe later."

"Saw on the weather channel there's a front movin' in. Perfect for the long weekend; at least the kids think so." He grinned, not minding the tobacco-stained teeth at all. "My wife's cookin' up a pot of clam chowder and homemade biscuits."

"Nice on a cold night."

"Ayuh." Miguel leaned his elbow on the counter. "What can I get for ya?"

"I'd like a pint of gin, please. Medium price range is fine."

His brow rose. "Gin is nice to add to a cup of joe. I've got some brewed in the back," he said leadingly.

She shook her head immediately. "No, no…it's a gift. Not for me."

"Oh, okay then." Miguel straightened. "No offense meant."

Small towns. Islands. This was how gossip started and spread. "I drink tea to relax." Riley didn't explain who the gin was for or offer more information. The news would beat her to

Nelson's house, if she did. Miguel wrapped it up for her in a small paper sack and she paid in cash.

"To each their own," Miguel said, scooting the bag to her, sounding as pious as a saint.

"You happen to know Lars Sorenson, by chance?"

Miguel's lips twitched. "Sure. Lars played poker with some of us real late Friday or Saturday nights, to the wee morning hours, sometimes, after he finished at The Shack. I thought he left for Bangor?"

"He did." Riley nodded but remained by the counter without picking up the bag of gin. This was confirmation that Lars liked his cards *and* had someone to play with.

"What's this about?" Miguel glanced toward his pack of cigarettes, Marlboro Red, and the lighter. A deck of cards was next to the smokes.

"I met him the other night, is all, at the Lobster Pot."

"He's in town?" Miguel's voice rose two octaves. Interesting.

Riley stayed in a relaxed pose. "Yep."

"I'd like to catch up with him. He's a damn cheater who owes me money and a wicked sore loser, too. Had to explain to the wife about my black eye when I called him on it. He was drunk as a skunk, though."

"When was this?"

"Dunno. Six months ago? I ain't good with time." Miguel sucked his awful teeth. "He probably don't even remember. Well, you see him, let him know I want a word."

"Did you file a formal complaint?"

"At the station?" Miguel looked at her like she'd lost her mind. "No. It was just a game."

"But he *punched* you."

Miguel shrugged it off though Riley could tell he was still miffed.

She studied Miguel discreetly. The man stocked his own boxes, if the biceps beneath the flannel shirt were anything to judge by. A flat silver box knife rested next to a jar of pens, the smokes, and the credit card machine.

"Do you fish?"

"Only when I have to," Miguel chuckled. "Other than my wife's clam chowder, I hate seafood. Give me beef any day."

Riley nodded and left, taking her brown bag of gin with her.

When she got in the SUV she checked to see if there was cell signal to set up an interview with Kimber. Nothing. Nothing from Matthew either.

How did people live like this?

The GPS directed her down the coastal road, away from the main streets and neighborhoods. The snow made driving a bit more of challenge, but after a few slick turns, she got the feel for the way the road handled beneath the tires.

She passed the marina, which was busy as the Murphys also sold groceries and hardware in addition to touristy items. The long weekend probably made the place busier since it was a holiday for so many people. There didn't seem to be many prepping for the storm.

They were used to snow, unlike Riley. All of this white was no big deal to them.

After ten minutes, Riley arrived at a group of twenty sheds in varying styles and ages. About five had new roofs. Half had chimneys indicating a bit more inside the shed than just a pallet and a shelf, like Matthew's grandpa'd had. The rest were forlorn and barely upright.

Nelson Bach had a sign that read Bach's Beach Paradise on a shingle, so Riley pulled in front of it and parked. Smoke drifted lazily upward into the gray sky. A sturdy gray tow truck was alongside the glorified shed—she would guess it to be about twelve by twelve. Hardly bigger than a tiny home, but it had a fabulous view of the bay.

Right now, the water was dark charcoal and choppy with whitecaps. The snow melted into the water as if it had no substance. On the ground, the snow had been heavy enough to form drifts and hold Lars's body.

Kitty-corner behind Nelson's place was a new "shed" that even had a doormat. She supposed that was all a single person would need. Could Lars have had one of his own down here?

She pulled the key from the ignition and exited the SUV. The path had been shoveled to the front door, so she followed it and knocked. Nelson answered and she was very glad that Matthew had given her a heads-up on his skinniness. He had red cheeks, silver hair, and jeans held up over bony hips with suspenders. He actually had his thick sweater tucked in.

"Nelson Bach?"

"Yeah?" He eyed her with wary confusion, recognizing the SUV and her uniform but not her per se. Her guess was that the cops coming to his door was never a good thing.

She offered the gin. "A thank you for towing my car to the auto shop. I'm Riley Harper. We haven't met yet since I've joined the department."

His expression cleared and Nelson accepted the brown bag. "No need, no need—but thanks. Wanna come in?"

Riley glanced around as if undecided, but then said, "Sure. I have to admit I'm very curious about your…" Would she offend him by calling it a shanty? "Abode?"

He cackled and widened the door. "Ah, we call 'em miracles. A strong wind should blow 'em over but they don't. We're in the curve of the coastline. It protects from the highest winds and provides amazing fishing, even when it's bitter cold."

"Oh!" That made sense. She nodded, glad for the explanation. "You inherited yours?"

"Ayuh. It's got to be in the family—you can't just decide to put one up willy-nilly."

Riley stepped inside a space the size of the kitchen in her rental. Nelson had a woodstove, a cot for a bed, a sink, and a counter with a hot plate.

It was cozy and warm and not at all claustrophobic because he had a sunlight in the roof and thin glass panes over the kitchen sink to let in the light.

"This is really nice."

"I like it." He brought the pint bottle from the brown paper bag. "Thanks for this—wanna shot?"

"Oh no. I'm in uniform."

"Ah." He smiled and waited for her to begin the conversation, eyeing the pint longingly.

Riley should've bought a larger size. "Do you happen to know when the car will be done?"

"Gary said he'd call but not to expect it before Tuesday." Nelson nodded toward the door alluding to the SUV. "I see you have another ride though."

"I do." She would have to come clean to the chief ASAP. Riley cleared her throat. "How many people live here full-time, do you think?"

"Two of us old-timers. And Charlie Higgins, if him and Joan are going at it." Nelson smoothed the label of the gin.

Riley laughed. "Did Lars Sorenson live around here?"

He took the cap off and sipped daintily like the bottle was a teacup. "No, ma'am, er Officer. Lars is no good, that one. The island was better off when he left. I hate to say it since I knew his granddad—passed twenty years or so, now. He's nothin' but trouble."

Riley added Nelson's obvious dislike of Lars to the pile of others who felt the same. "You played poker?"

"Yeah. Sure did." Nelson hooked a thumb around his suspenders.

"With Lars?"

He gave a clipped nod.

"And?"

"What?"

Nelson's cool demeanor led Riley to believe that the old man was probably a decent poker player no matter how much he drank. He only gave away what he wanted. She'd met guys like him before.

"Lars," she repeated. "Did he owe *you* money?"

"Not me."

"Anybody else, besides Miguel?"

"Miguel told you?" His voice showed a hint of surprise.

"Yep." She could play hardball. Miguel had said Lars had cheated, too.

Nelson took another sip and savored the gin, then decided to share. "Lars owed a lot of folks. Never got me though. I was onto him. Lars had a tell; you know what that is?"

Riley shook her head, though she did. She wanted to hear Nelson's version and keep him talking.

"It's when you're playing cards and you give somethin' away, when you're bluffin', like a tap of the finger to the table or a little twitch of the mouth." He drank again. "Lars had a tell that the others never caught on to."

"What was it?"

"I can't tell ya that!"

"How about for the *big* bottle of gin?" Riley asked.

His mouth quirked. "Make it two."

"Deal. You have to trust me that I'm good for it."

Nelson cocked his head. "All right. When Lars had a winning hand," he paused and looked around as if anybody could be hiding in the tiny space.

Riley waited, masking her impatience.

"He'd touch the spade tattoo on the knuckle of his forefinger."

"Is it that important?" Touching a tattoo didn't seem like much.

Nelson cackled and raised the gin bottle. "I'm the only one he hardly ever beat, so I'd say, yeah."

He had a point there.

"Who all used to play?" Riley asked.

Nelson shrugged. "Don't recall."

Uh huh. "Thank you for your time. I'll have Miguel deliver that gin to you, all right?"

Nelson grinned as he walked her out the door to the path. Another inch or two of snow had accumulated. "But no sharing the man's secrets, 'kay?"

Riley didn't have the authority to share that Lars's poker playing days were over.

CHAPTER SIX

R ILEY LEFT N ELSON B ACH'S SHANTY AND USED THE RADIO TO call Matthew at the station. Rosita answered instead.

"Hey, Riley. Matthew went out to the woods to follow Crash's route and see if there was an obvious place for Lars to be picked up and dragged." Rosita's voice caught. "That sounds so unfeeling."

"Death is never easy, Rosita," Riley said with empathy. "I've been on the job for fifteen years and it still stings." She checked the mirrors but there was nobody else on the road. She was used to the city where it didn't matter what time of day or night it was, there was light and people. "Do you have an ETA for Matthew to return?"

"No. Sorry. Are you on your way?"

Somehow it had gotten to be almost three in the afternoon. The sky was getting darker though the snow added an odd light illusion.

"Yes. I need to make another stop." The liquor store. "And I'm trying to reach Kimber, but I've had no luck. I'll pick up Tessa's information when I get there. What's going on over there?"

"Captain Wyatt said the forecasters still predict the nor'easter to wobble out to sea."

"Really?" Riley was mesmerized by the fall of flakes against the windshield. "But it hasn't stopped snowing."

"This is normal." Rosita chuckled. "You'll get used to it."

Riley wasn't sure about that. Even if she could, would Kyra? She imagined her family at home and her heart gave a ping. She missed them and needed hugs to banish the dark.

Her duty to find a killer took precedence over family time. She imagined that they'd be pulling a late night at the station. "Do you have Kimber's address?"

"I can find it for you. Anything else? I should probably clock out once you get here. I'm already over my scheduled hours for the week."

"Oh. Let me come back then so you can leave."

"No rush." But her tone suggested that Riley not dawdle.

Riley stopped at the liquor store and paid Miguel to deliver two large bottles of gin to Nelson Bach. "I hear that Nelson is practically a card sharp," she said.

Miguel snorted and tapped a king card outside the deck. The scent of tobacco flared through his nostrils. "Oh yeah? In his gin-soaked mind maybe."

They shared a smile. "Do you happen to know of anyone else that Lars would consider a mate? A girlfriend or hookup, even?"

"He always talked about the ladies, if you know what I mean, but never anybody serious. Lars was a player and liked it that way."

Which meant that the bar was the perfect job for him, with fresh tourists in all summer. She left and tried to call Coby—the cell phone actually connected and Coby answered, "Hello!"

"Coby, it's Riley. Officer Harper. Do you know if Lars had a suitcase, or bag? I—"

She was talking into dead air.

Riley gritted her teeth and dropped the frustrating phone to the center console. The snowy weather required slow driving and it was four when she at last arrived at the police station. Matthew's sedan was parked next to Rosita's Jeep. She hurried in the back door.

"What a day," she announced, dropping the keys to the center of the table.

Rosita was packing up for the night. "It has been rough. I'll see you guys on Tuesday since I have the next two days off. Unless you need me to come in but then we should clear it with the chief."

"I'll talk to him, if you're willing to help out," Matthew said. "We are nowhere on this case." He looked at Riley with hope in his eyes. "Unless you solved it?"

"I did not." She unzipped her jacket.

"I stocked up on frozen pizza," Rosita said, "when it was on sale last month so there are three in the freezer if you need dinner. Frozen veggies. Nothing gourmet but it will fill your bellies. Tessa Barton's information is on your desk, Riley, and Kimber's addy."

"Thank you. Rosita, do you mind stopping by my place and checking on my family?" Riley met the other woman's gaze and allowed a little of her heart show. "Let them know I'll be home around eight or so. I'm a bit worried about them."

Rosita's face brightened at having something to do. "I will—but this is normal," she stressed, repeating the same word she'd used before. "Promise." She put her hand to her chest.

"Thanks."

Once Rosita left, she and Matthew exhaled and both started talking at once. Laughing, Riley held up her hand to speak.

"Fine. You first," Matthew said.

"Let's call the chief."

"No cell service."

She uttered a phrase she was beginning to hate. "Let's radio the chief."

Matthew nodded and turned on the oven to preheat. Riley got out a supreme frozen pizza and set it on the counter. They spent the next three minutes going over what they knew and what they didn't. According to Crash's route on the map, Lars's body could have been picked up in a mile radius from the woods. It was doubtful that it had been buried in the ditch near Coby's house. They put the pizza in, and then Riley led the way to the radio console at the workstations behind Nancy's desk.

She turned on the machine, dialed the chief, and pressed the button on the handheld mic.

"Harper to Barnes. Harper to Barnes."

As if he'd been expecting them the chief answered immediately. "Barnes here. Any news?"

"That's why we're calling you," Riley said. "For news. Did you speak with the doctor?"

"Dr. Lakshmi has been busy today with emergencies of the living, she told me. Quite curtly."

Riley bit her lip. Matthew's shoulder shook, but both of them were quiet.

Static crackled, then Barnes said, "She'll try to get to it tomorrow but fears that forcing the hand open might destroy evidence, so we need to be patient."

Lars was on defrost until then. Riley shrugged at Matthew.

"The storm makes it near impossible to get home right now so I need you two to do me proud and find the killer. The weather is covering up clues which doesn't help." Barnes's tone implied that he wasn't sure they were up to the task.

"We will do our best," Riley said, and Matthew agreed.

Riley then went over everything that they'd discovered though there were so many leads still to follow.

"It's a start," Barnes said. "Once it's dark, I know you'll be stuck so you may need to get a really early start in the morning."

"We can do that." Riley tapped the desk. "Uh, sir, I need to tell you about the Fiat."

"Yeah?"

"It's in the shop. So, I'm using your SUV until it's out on Tuesday. Otherwise, I would be useless to you, with Matthew having to drive me around everywhere."

She could feel his tension and annoyance, but then he blew out an explosive breath. "Fine. There better not be a scratch on it."

"No, sir."

"And, sir?" Matthew interjected. "Rosita knows about Lars. Can we call her in to assist if we need to? She would be over her scheduled hours."

"You both give me a headache. How can I be away for a few days if you can't figure this stuff out? No telling anybody else about Lars being dead. Let's touch base in the morning."

At that, Chief Barnes was no longer on the radio call.

Riley exhaled, having feared being written up over the SUV incident but he'd handled it okay. They sort of had approval for Rosita if they needed her to come in and answer phones so she and Matthew could do their jobs in the field.

They smacked hands but then jumped as the smoke alarm went off in the kitchen. Matthew darted ahead with Riley on his heels. Smoke billowed from the oven.

Matthew waved his hand before his nose to clear the smoke and turned on the overhead fan, rescuing the crisp pizza from inside.

Riley collapsed at the table with laughter. "I hate to think about what's coming next. My heart can't take it."

Despite the burned pepperoni, Riley and Matthew divided the pie and worked on the whiteboard in the lunchroom. Riley wondered what kind of crimes had been solved on that blank board. "What do we know? Let's start from the beginning."

Matthew uncapped a pen and wrote Lars Sorenson on the board. "Thirty. Bartender with a drinking problem. Thief. Fighter. We need to find out who he was playing poker with."

"Miguel and Nelson, for sure." She drummed her lip with her fingernail. "He had a thing for the ladies. We've heard that from a lot of folks, starting with Kimber."

Matthew tossed her a different color pen. "You write down persons of interest." He scooted to the right so she could take the left side.

"Kimber." Riley hated to do it, but she had to. "Ryker. Emily? She works on karaoke nights."

"Add her to the list. Coby as well," Matthew said hesitantly. "They had a past. I can hear the chief now, yelling that we need to clear Coby with logic, not our instincts."

She added the name, her nose scrunched. "I can't see Coby that out of control. Sure Lars had broken into his safe and he'd feel violated, but not to this extent."

Matthew rubbed his chin. "This morning, I'd never seen Coby so riled up."

Riley lowered her pen as they stared at one another. "You don't...think?" Coby...

"Nah!" Matthew flushed. "Coby was just furious that his safe was broken into."

She traced the map of Crash's route near Coby's house. A few blocks over. Along the woods.

Matthew traded his pen for pizza, chewed, and swallowed—his gaze intent on their board.

"We can't traipse through Mackabee Woods tonight, but we should tomorrow," Riley said. "See if we can find anything. The Hamiltons' home butts up against part of the forest."

"All right. It won't be easy, but we can give it a shot—dress warm!"

"What did Bernie ever say about the boat?"

"Nothing. I asked Sally to have him call me, but she said it was really busy at the marina."

"There are days I wish the detecting process was a straight line," Riley commented. "Instead of all over the place." She called

Tessa's number, but it rang and rang. Riley copied the address and phone number on a scrap paper and stuck it in her jacket, along with Kimber's.

At seven that evening, while they were still going over plans for the next day, the station phone rang. Riley raced for Nancy's phone on the receptionist's desk. It could be her mom or an islander in trouble. She prayed the call wouldn't be about another dead body.

"Officer Harper."

"Hi, Riley? It's Kimber! You left a message?"

"Yes." Riley preferred to do interviews in person rather than over the phone because you could see more if you watched the person talk. Their body language revealed as much as their words. "I'd love to stop by your place tomorrow and talk for a few minutes."

"About what?" Kimber's tone became guarded.

"Working at The Shack. I have a few questions." Riley didn't say Lars, specifically.

Kimber giggled. "You looking for part-time work? You're better than The Shack."

Riley laughed along with her. "I'll explain tomorrow. What time's good for you?"

"Tamara and I will be home tomorrow working on our crocheted blankets so stop by anytime." Kimber reeled off her address—it matched what Riley already had.

"Thanks. See you then." Riley turned to Matthew, suddenly exhausted. "All right. That was Kimber. We set up a time for tomorrow. We've accomplished a lot tonight. Ready to call it quits?"

He nodded and started collecting the paper plates and napkins they'd used to throw in the trash. "Let's head out then and meet here tomorrow at eight. Any earlier and we won't be able to see."

"Good job, partner."

They locked up the station and each drove home. Riley arrived at the rental, the chief's SUV easily handling the plowed roads. They'd had about four feet. The snow had stopped and the night was beautiful.

She went inside and the coziness of the fire and the hugs of greeting from her mom and her daughter banished the darkness of Lars's death.

***

RILEY WOKE at seven the next day and dressed in her Sandpiper Bay winter uniform of thick navy-blue pants, black socks, and boots. She'd learned quickly that she needed layers up top—silk against her skin to absorb the moisture without trapping it, then fleece, her uniform shirt, and finally her jacket.

The key was to stay warm but still be mobile. Too thick and she couldn't draw a weapon or even drive the car. As she went down the stairs to the kitchen, Riley felt like the marshmallow man in *Ghostbusters*. She planned on making coffee at the station to be quiet so that her family wouldn't wake up.

Riley went out the front, following the path Kyra had shoveled to the road. The gray sky had dumped another foot of thick flakes. She couldn't believe how shockingly white it was on the island, like Mother Nature had dumped confectioner's sugar over the pine trees and houses. The sound of the seagulls was eerily out of place and the chittering squirrels seemed angry.

Where did the wildlife go during a storm?

Maybe the same place Lars's killer had hidden out. Mackabee Woods.

Riley spotted two men in snowshoes coming down the hill. She waited until they arrived, stopping near the porch.

"Hey, guys. You're up early." Carter and Don both had ruddy complexions from the chilly air, though Don's blue eyes sparkled at her as he grinned.

"Matthew stopped by our place this morning," Carter said. "He asked us to check on you to make sure you still had power this morning."

She took half a step back at Don's friendly grin. "We do. Thanks."

"Where are you off to?" Don asked.

"The station. We have a missing persons case we're working on."

Carter brought out a bag with three walkie talkies. "I don't know that they'll reach from your house to the department, but for around here, they should be good. We're just a mile away and I bet Kyra and your mom can reach us if they need to for anything."

"Thank you!"

Don shuffled his snowshoes. "If you lose power again, sometimes it's because the generator freezes up and you just need to knock the snow off. Is it gas or battery?"

"Gas." Which she only knew because Matthew had told her.

"You might need to change the tank," Don said. "You know how to do that?"

She thought about lying for all of two seconds but then the idea of her family being blown sky high because of her misplaced pride made her admit, "No. But I'll learn. Can you show me real quick?"

Don swept his wool hat off and ran his fingers through his curly brown hair. "I'd be happy to."

Ten minutes later, she understood the basics of the generator and how to change the tank. If she found Don attractive, who could blame her?

She checked the time on her watch. Quarter till eight. She started walking toward the SUV and opened the door.

Don trailed her, obviously wanting to chitchat. "A missing person, huh?"

Riley banished the image of Lars and gave Don a friendly smile. "Yeah."

"But you can't talk about it?"

She nodded.

"I always wanted to be a police officer when I grew up, but then I became a lawyer instead." Don's eyes were deep blue and dark curls waved around his forehead and to his ears. It was a professional styled cut but only added to his attractiveness.

"You're still working with the law. What kind of attorney?"

"I specialize in family law though I started off as defense for a cutthroat firm. I learned pretty quick that it wasn't for me."

Riley stuffed her cold hands into her pockets. Another minute or two wouldn't kill her.

In Phoenix, she'd been blacklisted by her old friends, so it had been a while since a man had shown interest in her. Don was smart and compassionate to leave the money in defense law for family care.

"You're happy?"

"Oh yes. And I can look at myself in the mirror." He laughed.

"The best decision then," Riley agreed, scuffing her work boots in the snow. Family was important to him. "You have kids?"

"Nope. I was married after college for a few years, but children never happened for us. It worked out for the best since we split." He shrugged.

"I am also divorced—happily divorced at that."

Don chuckled. "So, do you mind if I get your phone number? I'd like to take you to dinner sometime."

Riley's cheeks flushed. "Oh, well..." Why not? She was divorced. She liked dinner. And Don was very cute. "I'm not looking for anything but friendship. Is that all right?"

"Slow is my middle name." Don held up his palm like he was swearing on the Bible in court.

She laughed. "Then yes. I'll give you my cell number later—right now I need to get to the station."

Don whipped out his phone. "Let me add it real quick—unless you're trying to blow me off?"

"I'm not." She gave it to him, her stomach twirling. "Slow." Riley got into the SUV and started the engine.

Matthew radioed her as she drove, interrupting her daydreams of a candlelit dinner with Don somewhere romantic. "Riley, you there? It's Matthew."

"Here!"

The radio crackled. "I'm at the station, Riley. How soon can you get here?"

"On my way—what's wrong?" They'd agreed to be at work at eight and it was only ten till.

"Ryker Hamilton is missing."

Her insides froze as she drew up the picture of the gawky fifteen-year-old at the Hamilton house. He'd been cocky, but likeable.

"How long?"

"The parents just discovered him gone. Saw him around eleven last night. Sam sounded frantic."

"Trust me, I would be too." She sucked in a breath. If something bad ever happened to Kyra, she'd never forgive herself, and she would do anything to save her.

"As soon as you get here, we can go together to the Hamiltons."

"See you in ten."

Matthew was waiting outside, dressed in his warm jacket; his breath plumed as he stomped his feet. She parked and got out.

"Ryker is a kid who thinks very highly of himself—to his detriment," Matthew said. "I hope he hasn't done anything stupid."

Riley nodded, recalling his ease with the air rifle. "Let's go."

Matthew cranked opened the door of the blue sedan and got in, starting the car. Riley slid in the passenger side.

His wholesome face had become dear to her over the last few months. She'd never known anyone so genuine.

"All right," she said as Matthew backed up, the rear sliding a bit in the snow. "Ryker. Fifteen. Do you think he left on his own will? Was he trying to find Lars? You think he had something to do with his death?"

"Whoa!" Matthew said, keeping his eyes on the slick road ahead of them. "He's a kid. So, no. That's not even on my radar."

She thought of the list of serial killers that were children but didn't press the point.

"Have you talked to Coby this morning?" Riley asked. Both she and Matthew trusted him as an honest man; he was a friend.

Matthew shook his head, a smile appearing briefly before his serious expression returned. "It's only eight! Coby is a night owl."

"When did you find out about Ryker?"

"An hour ago. Sam drove his snowmobile to my house and woke me up. If they're asking for assistance, they're worried. The Hamiltons are independent with a capital *I*. They saw their son last at around eleven last night. They all went to bed after a family card game. Sam got up this morning to let the puppy out and noticed that Ryker wasn't in his room or in the house."

"That's why you were up so early, sending Carter and Don to check on me. Thanks, by the way. I now know how to change the gas tank without blowing us to the moon." She glanced at Matthew with a half-smile. "You didn't tell them about Lars, did you?"

"No. Chief said to keep it under wraps. I happen to like my job."

Gossip spread fast on a small island, though, as she'd learned. "Do you feel like Sam knew more about it?"

"About what?"

Sam Hamilton had been very protective of his family, and he hadn't liked Lars one bit. Had offered to drop him off in the middle of the ocean. "That Lars didn't disappear. That he's dead."

"Geez, Riley. I really don't know. And I hate having to doubt my friends."

"There are no friends in a criminal investigation." Another lesson Riley had learned the hard way.

CHAPTER SEVEN

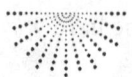

BEFORE THEY TURNED OFF THE MAIN ROAD, RILEY SHOUTED FOR Matthew to stop. "We've got cell signal! Hurry." She called Chief Barnes, whose voice sounded hoarse like they'd woken him up.

Riley quickly brought him up to speed.

"Look, I'm real sorry Ryker is missing. Hopefully he'll be sitting at the breakfast table by the time you arrive."

"We hope so too, sir." Riley pulled on the seat belt which dug in her shoulder when Matthew continued to drive. "What do you know of Sam Hamilton?"

Barnes cleared his throat. "You're barking up the wrong tree if you think this family has anything to do with Lars Sorenson. I've given this some thought, and Coby Jenkins was the last person to see him that night. That's a fact. It's also a fact that he's had a few run-ins with him—before the jerk up and quit, leaving Coby shorthanded. Lars wanted payback."

"Chief." Riley winced as heavy snow fell from a tree limb to the windshield. Matthew kept perfect control. "I hear what you're saying but what would Coby gain by killing Lars?"

"Dang if I know. Why does anyone murder anyone? Gotta

have a lot of hatred to choke a person like that. Sure can't see Sam or that boy Ryker doing something so vile."

Seemed like Chief Barnes had a favorite, and it wasn't Coby. "We'll tread lightly."

"Do that when you talk to them. Maybe the meandering son has found his way back."

"That would be a lucky break. Last thing we need is two bodies piled up," Matthew responded. Just then, the call dropped.

Riley was used to more reliable communication.

She pointed to the folks crowded around the front porch and pictures windows of the Hamilton home. "Looks like they might have family or friends here already to help search. Word gets around quick."

"It's small-town community," Matthew said proudly.

People stood near the doorway, talking quietly among themselves. She recognized Crash, thanks to his big dog Shazam, and Trevor, the paramedic. Charlie Higgins. He'd opened the back of his truck and had donuts and boxes of coffee with small paper cups. Matthew nodded and they made room for the officers, watching with interest.

Riley met Trevor's curious gaze. "Any word on Ryker?"

Trevor shook his head sadly. "Nope. Waiting for a bit and then we plan on scouring the woods."

"Before you do that," Riley said, thinking of clues that could be trampled, "please let us talk to the family."

Matthew rapped on the door. He was about to do it again, when one guy said, "Walk in. Everyone's hanging around the table and the phone, some out back. Hoping and praying just like us. I'm Randy. This is my wife, Carol."

The couple was bundled up and had matching blue scarves and gloves. "I'm Officer Harper. Can you think of anything that might help locate Ryker? His friends, who he liked to go hiking with?"

"Ryker's a good kid—most of the time. You know how teens get. All uppity, think they know everything and that their parents are unenlightened human beings who lived in the dark ages, before everything got cool." Carol shrugged her thin shoulders. "Can't blame them, I suppose. I used to be one of those kids." Her round face lit with a smile. "But he and Frankie are best friends. Dorian too. Lindsay and Sam will tell you."

Riley knew all too well what she was talking about. "My girl's fourteen, I get it."

"Thanks for talking with us," Matthew said, holding the door for Riley to enter.

They headed toward the kitchen where angry and frightened voices clamored to be heard. Riley swallowed hard, thinking how she'd be out of her mind right now if it was Kyra not in her bed.

"Good morning," she said quietly to the crowd who'd gathered. She knew the Hamiltons and Serge out of the ten in the kitchen. "I'm Officer Harper, and you all probably know Officer Sniders. We'd like to ask a few questions to help find Ryker."

Lindsay cried into a dish towel as a woman comforted her with a half hug. "I'm sure he's on his way home now, hon."

Riley truly hoped so. Until then, they had a job to do. The group of friends said hasty goodbyes, then drifted away.

Matthew had a hand on Sam's back as the handsome strong father tried to hold his grief in. He was visibly shaking and looked frightened to death. What loving dad wouldn't be?

Lindsay had red swollen eyes and was clinging to a box of tissues as if it were her life support. The dark-blond hair was uncombed, sheltering her downturned face.

With a gentle touch, Riley led her to a sofa in the living room and sat next to her, holding her hands. The black puppy had a lowered tail as if it knew something was wrong.

"I'm so sorry. I have a daughter around the same age as your son, and I'd be frantic too. But it is far too soon to think the worst. Most likely he'll walk in any moment and have quite an explanation handy."

Lindsay glanced up with a flicker of hope in her tortured gaze. "Yes, he will. I'm sure he will." Bear scrambled from the living room to sniff at the stairs, then joined Sam in the kitchen. Where was Emily?

"Do you mind answering a few questions?"

Taking another tissue from the box, Lindsay nodded her consent.

Riley brought out her stylus and opened her notes on her phone. "Who is he hanging out with? Does he have a best friend?"

"Frankie Sharpe. The two are like brothers."

Riley recalled the ease that Ryker had held the air rifle. "Do they go to the woods with their air rifles?"

"Yes, of course. But I already called Shamara, Frankie's mom. Ryker isn't there, and Frankie's fast asleep."

"Who else?"

Sighing, she said, "Dorian Washburne. They've been palling around more. I'll call his mom."

"Good. Would Ryker go to the woods by himself?"

Lindsay shredded her tissue. "Sure. But not at night. That place can be creepy. We trust him…"

And yet, Ryker was gone. Riley cleared her throat, not judging but empathetic. "The world's become such a dangerous place. Kids used to be able to go to the local parks by themselves, hang out together until their parents called them in for dinner."

A little smile crept to the corners of Lindsay's mouth. "It's still like that here on the island."

"Fifteen-year-old boys don't always think of safety first. Do they?"

"No." Lindsay dabbed her nose with her crumpled tissue. "Ryker struts around these days like he's all that. It was amusing until lately, but now I worry that he might grow up to be a reckless man if he doesn't change his ways."

"How is that?" Riley patted Lindsay's knee. "I only ask because it's those seemingly unimportant details that often lead to a bigger clue."

"Well, he wanted an air rifle for his fifteenth birthday, and we caved in because Frankie also has one. Mackabee's is only half a mile from here. Sam taught them how to track—he's really good."

Riley nodded encouragingly. Ryker was comfortable in the woods nearby the place Lars had been found.

Just then a crash sounded from upstairs. Glass shattered. Riley jumped up and looked at the staircase. Matthew and Sam entered the living room. Sam was on the first step, holding the puppy by the collar.

"Ryker?" Sam called.

Bear whined. "Bed," Sam ordered. The dog, head down, went to the large cushion in the living room and Matthew joined Riley at the couch.

Relief spread across Lindsay's features before she followed her husband and went upstairs to what Riley assumed was Ryker's bedroom.

Matthew murmured to Riley, "You got anything?"

"Maybe. Ryker is very competent as a survivalist in the woods. He's got an air rifle. Sam taught Ryker and his best buddy how to track in the forest. Could be typical teenage behavior." She smirked at Matt. "Like your wild youth."

"Don't remind me." His freckles stood out on his red face. "We need to question Ryker more closely."

"I agree. Let's see how the parents handle this and decide to do it now or later today."

"Have you seen Emily?" Matthew whispered. They walked shoulder to shoulder toward the staircase and looked up.

Ryker's voice was intermittent with his parents. At least he was home.

Riley shook her head. "Weird, isn't it? No way could she sleep through the commotion. Surely her parents woke her to ask if she'd seen him. Why stay upstairs?"

Sam, mouth tight, arrived at the top of the staircase. "He's back. Sorry I got you both out here so early in the morning." He walked slowly down the steps. "As you pointed out, it was too soon to panic." He clapped Matthew on the back. "Appreciate you rushing out here even if it was for nothing."

"No problem. While we're here can we have a word..."

Matthew's sentence was cut short when Lindsay—her hand on her son's shoulder—trotted down the stairs where they all crowded by the sofa. "Ryker wants to apologize to you both."

Head down, obviously uncomfortable, Ryker grumbled an apology, not looking them in the eye. He had brambles in his hair and scratches on his face, fitting for someone who'd spent the night in the woods. How could he have survived a night outside in this weather?

Lindsay shoved her hands in her pockets with a stern expression, stepping between Matthew and Ryker.

"Glad you're back," Matthew said to the teen. "Don't scare your parents like that again unless you want to see our friendly faces here more often. Where did you go?"

"The woods."

"Alone?" Riley asked. She brought out her phone to take notes.

She was surprised when he said, "Yeah."

"What?" Lindsay swiveled toward Ryker and placed her hand on his forearm. "Why?"

Ryker gave a sheepish grin. "I was just curious what it would be like to sleep outside. We love that show, *Alone*," he told Matthew and Riley. "Snow was falling so thick and fast—like a blanket dropping from the sky covering everything in white. I got lost trying to come back. Nearly froze my butt off too. Think I might have frostbite." He held his hands out for them to see.

"And what?" Riley studied his boots and clothes again. Damp but not soaked. "You waited until dawn to make it home?"

"I hunkered down somewhere." Ryker didn't meet her gaze. Interesting. How to get this kid by himself and interview him?

Sam raised one of Ryker's hands, then the other. "Bluish tips." He tapped the ends. "You feel that?"

Ryker's chin quivered. "It's numb, but tingly too."

Sam's jaw clenched. "We'll keep an eye on those. Where were you, son, exactly?"

"I found a natural cave just big enough for me to slip in sideways with my back to the curve of the wall. I remembered what we learned on season five of *Alone*, about being warm, so I carpeted the place with pine boughs and leaves to cut the wind and stay dry."

Matthew arched a ginger brow. "That's smart thinking."

"I hate that show," Lindsay said, tears in her voice and her eyes as she studied her son. "It pushes people to think they're superhuman. What kind of idiot risks their lives against the elements for half a million bucks?"

Riley didn't know what they were talking about—but people would do a lot for that kind of money. "I saw Trevor Dunfield outside," she said. "He's a paramedic and would know what to do. What me to call him in?"

"We can handle things from here, thank you anyway, Officer Harper," Sam said. He exuded anger and relief as he kept his gaze on his son. "Thanks, Matthew."

"No problem." Matthew glanced at Riley. "Anything you'd like to know before we go?"

She shifted to Ryker, wondering if he was telling the entire truth. "Is there any other reason you might have gone into the woods last night?"

"My kids don't lie, Officer Harper." Sam tore his gaze from Ryker to her. He was king in his house and wanted her to know it. "I told you that before."

"I wanted to sleep alone outside," Ryker repeated. The black puppy left the cushion to sniff around the teenager's legs.

"My brother is cra-azy," Emily said as she appeared at the top of the stairs, fully made up and dressed for the day. "Sounds like something dumb he'd do. Surprised you didn't take your dog."

Where was Emily going? Riley wondered. Her jeans had holes at the knees, fur-lined boots hit mid-calf, and a bulky fur vest covered a ribbed turtleneck. Mascara and lipstick at eight in the morning?

"Good morning, Emily," her mother spoke with a little heat. "I thought you didn't feel well?"

Emily descended the stairs, ignoring her mother, and the fact that there were officers in her living room.

"Can you leave your brother alone? He's had a rough night." Lindsay retrieved a blanket from the couch to wrap around Ryker's shoulders.

"Sorryyy..." Emily sauntered into the kitchen. "Can't believe you guys freaked out. Ryker learned how to survive from Dad. Here, Bear!" The dog raced after her as she gave him a treat.

"Officers? I'd like to be with my family right now, if you don't mind..." Sam gestured toward the front door.

Riley nodded, not taking offense but wishing they could get Ryker alone for a while. Was Emily taking his side?

They walked outside into the cold. Crash and Trevor were joking around with Charlie by the back of his truck, but the other neighbors had gone. The men were all bundled up for the weather. Trevor walked over to them with a grin. "We saw Ryker shimmy up the tree by his window. Everything okay?"

"Looks that way," Riley said.

"They're watching his fingers for frostbite," Matthew

explained further. "How'd you hear about Ryker being missing so fast?"

Crash and Charlie joined them with nods of hello. She knew Charlie of course but hadn't officially met Crash.

"Officer Harper," she said as they shook hands. His big dog Shazam lounged by Charlie's back wheel, possibly hoping for donut crumbs. His fur was thick and if she had to guess, she'd say the dog was a wolf mixed with German shepherd.

"Crash Moreno."

It was difficult not to ask the driver a million questions. When would Chief Barnes give them the all-clear?

"I'm up early at the bakery," Charlie explained, "and I saw Sam on the snowmobile, looking around for Ryker. He told me that his son was missing, and I called my pals. There's a storm about to hit, according to the forecasters."

"I thought it was going to wobble?" Riley asked. She hated that her voice rose slightly and hoped nobody noticed.

Trevor grunted. "It's a fifty-fifty chance but I can smell it in the air, and I wager we're gonna have at least a hundred mile an hour winds."

"Tonight?" Riley asked.

"Yeah." Trevor saw her face. "You'll be fine. But anybody in those shanties might end up in the middle of town. Don't you have one, Charlie? I know you do, Crash."

Both men nodded.

"Me and Crash don't live in ours, like Nelson," Charlie said. "I'll go check on him." He eyed the gray sky just as snow started to fall. "You'll be too busy on the plow today, Crash."

Crash shrugged and snapped his fingers, the sound muffled by leather gloves. "Shazam!" The big pup lumbered up and went to Crash's side. "You're probably right. Guess we better get a move on."

Riley asked, "Do you drive the same route, or does it vary?"

"I'm a creature of habit," Crash laughed. "I've been driving these roads for over twenty years." He smiled at them all, then patted Shazam. "Everyone, hang on tonight, and we'll see you on the other side."

Man and dog ambled off toward the woods.

Trevor said, "There's a shortcut along the trees to his cabin—not a shanty; the place has plumbing and everything." He winked.

Riley gratefully accepted a paper cup of coffee from Charlie to warm her. "There's really going to be that big of a storm *tonight?*"

"Trevor's got great instincts for these things, so yeah, I wouldn't take that bet." Charlie pulled a knit cap from his pocket and put it on.

She finished the small cup which was lukewarm after being out in the cold. "So what happens? Is there an alert or something that we need to put out to the people who live here?"

Matthew nudged her with his elbow. "Folks here know the drill. They'll have supplies from canned food to batteries. Rosita can make the rounds to check on those families who might not have enough to see them through."

"We'll call her from the station." Riley nodded to Charlie and Trevor. Charlie shut the back of his truck and said goodbye.

Trevor walked with her to the passenger side of the sedan. "Any news?" he asked quietly. "I haven't said anything and neither has Serge."

"Thanks," she said. "No. Not yet."

"You take care, now." Trevor swept snow from the top of the car. "And good luck."

Riley got inside and Matthew behind the wheel, turning the engine. Heat fogged the windshield.

"What was that about?" Matthew asked.

"Trevor was just asking if we'd found anything out about Lars. They said they hadn't said anything."

"Okay. Good. I saw your face about the storm. We don't

know for sure yet, all right? Let's call Wyatt. I trust him more than Trevor."

"How come?"

"Trevor's a gambler." Matthew grinned. "But Captain Wyatt has a sonar."

"Practical!" Riley chuckled. "We can also ask him what time Lars came over on the ferry, and whether or not he had a vehicle."

Matthew got the car moving and within minutes they were back on the main road. The heater was on full blast, and they took it slow back to the station so they could go over what they knew.

"Did you hear Crash say that he follows the same route?" Riley asked. "A creature of habit."

Matthew nodded. "Yeah. Let's follow Park Road by the woods and check out where Crash might have caught Lars in his plow. I think it could be the crossroads of Main and Park."

"All right." While they drove, Riley said, "Sam has survivalist skills that he's taught Ryker. Now, the kid is smart enough to survive outdoors in a snowstorm. And Emily was taking the heat off Ryker."

Matthew flipped on the wipers to bat away the snowflakes.

Riley asked, "Why would Emily cover for Ryker?"

"It's a sibling thing… My sisters would do it for me, and me for them. On the flip side, we could also turn on each other to get the heat off from our parents."

Riley removed her gloves and leaned by the door to see her partner's expressions. "I'm an only child. I always wanted a sibling."

"They can be your best friend and your worst enemy, until another enemy comes along," Matthew said with a laugh. "Then it's you against them."

She chuckled at the image of a ginger-haired sweet-faced army. "Is it too early to stop by the ferry depot and talk to

Captain Wyatt?" The idea of an actual storm coming with hurricane force winds didn't make her feel at all safe.

"Normally no, but he's probably not there since the ferry's docked."

"Oh. Shoot."

"Not to worry. He lives in the house a half block away. We can call from the station and have him meet us there."

When they neared Coby's, on Anchorage Street, they backtracked from where they'd found Lars. Snow and traffic had completely obliterated any clues.

He led them down Crash's route to a section of Mackabee Woods along Park Road, pulled over, and parked.

The two trudged through four feet of snow but between the plow and drifts and snowmobile tracks, there was nothing Riley could discern. Disappointed, she turned back about twenty minutes later. "I'd really hoped we'd learn something here."

Matthew tugged his hat down to protect his eyes. "I know. We're in a race against time. *If* the storm is coming, we'll be even more behind."

"With more clues buried under all of this." She gestured to the winter wonderland.

Riley stomped back to the car and got in. Sam had driven a snowmobile to find Matthew this morning. Could he have destroyed any tracks or clues on purpose?

"I saw how you were with Lindsay and Sam. You're really good with people." Matthew patted the steering wheel after starting the engine, then he joined the light traffic on the road. "Did you always know you wanted to be a cop?"

"Pretty much. I love the excitement and reward of keeping the civilian population safe from criminals. Discovering the who, the why, and the where is like putting the last piece on the puzzle. It's very satisfying solving a mystery. Outsmarting the guilty party. And they call us heroes"—she closed her eyes for a moment thinking back to her once illustrious career—"for serving justice and putting the bad guys in the slammer. What about you?"

"Yup. My dad was close friends with Chief LaSpada from thirty years ago, and I grew up with him taking care of our town. I wanted that feeling of serving our community. We need to find whoever killed Lars." Matthew stiffened his shoulders. "This is my island, and nobody messes with the innocent that live here or they will answer to me."

CHAPTER EIGHT

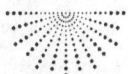

Buoyed by warm camaraderie, Riley was quiet in her thoughts as Matthew drove them back to the station. It was nice to have the respect of her fellow officer. Solving this murder before the clues were lost would certainly gain Chief Barnes's approval.

They went inside the empty building from the front entrance. It wasn't quite ten on Sunday, but she felt like she'd put in a full day because they'd started so early, added to the drama of Ryker being gone. She was just glad the teen was home safe.

"After Captain Wyatt, should we call the medical center?" Riley asked. "I have no idea how long it takes a body to unthaw."

"Chief said he'd handle it, so let's give it a few more hours." Matthew peeled his gloves off and then his coat, tossing them on Nancy's empty desk.

"All right. I want to know what was in Lars's hand… Any details the doc finds will help solve this crime." Riley unzipped her thick jacket and stuffed her gloves in the pockets before shrugging it off. "I have an interview with Kimber today, and I want to talk with Tessa. She's still not answering her phone. Maybe she's out of town?"

"For the holiday?" Matthew headed toward the breakroom. "We still haven't discovered *where* he was killed. There was no blood in the drift or on his body."

The falling snow covered everything so fast. "Did you notice all the snowmobile tracks around the woods? I'm worried the evidence will disappear in the worsening weather." Riley followed him down the hall and switched on the overhead light. "Where did he go after leaving Coby's house?"

Matthew glared at the whiteboard. "Lars was dressed when he left and had money he'd stolen from Coby."

"Yet he was naked when we found him." Riley rubbed a knot between her brows. "Clothes. Wallet. Phone. Where are those?"

Matthew crossed his arms and stepped back. "Drugs? If Lars was a junkie, he could have sold everything for a fix," Matthew suggested. "We can ask the doctor."

"Even his clothes? I don't know... I didn't see track marks, but that doesn't mean anything these days." Riley brushed her hands together. "I have an interview with Kimber today, and I might just drop by Tessa's since we have her address." She preferred to conduct interviews in person anyway.

"Good idea," Matthew agreed.

Riley tapped the map of the area Matthew had attached to the board. "Tessa's boarding house is only a few blocks from Coby's place. Have you talked to him?"

"Coby's been MIA. Probably at work. Doesn't matter the weather, the bar is almost always open."

"That means we can drop in and ask about the overnight bag or suitcase. Lars must have had something if he'd planned on staying in Sandpiper Bay." Riley stepped back. "What did Captain Wyatt say?"

"No answer. I left a message. Let me ask Bernie if he saw Lars the night he died." Matthew reached for the landline, but Riley stopped him with her hand on his forearm.

"Not until we get the chief's okay about letting people know Lars is dead."

He grimaced. "It's hampering the investigation."

Riley felt his frustration. "You can ask when the last time he'd seen Lars was, as he's missing. Also, Coby had suggested that Bernie might have names of people Lars played cards with." Seeing his expression she said, "I'd be surprised if they didn't already know. People are involved in this community. Did you see all the folks ready to help search for Ryker despite the cold? Charlie had even brought coffee."

"Would those same people have volunteered to look for Lars?" Matthew shook his head to answer his own question. He crossed his arms and scowled. "I hate waiting. Once I hear from Wyatt, I'll track down Coby and we can fill in our timeline of where Lars was, when."

Riley eyed the clock. "I should get going. I'll drive to Tessa's and then Kimber's. Do I need anything special for the storm? Like, taping the windows as you did at the Lobster Pot?"

"No. You're going to be fine. *If* it happens, it will be extremely loud and terrifying, but the generator is all set up. You've got firewood and food. Water."

She shivered. What would she tell her family? "Okay. Thanks." Riley retrieved the chief's SUV keys. "I'll be in touch."

"Keep your radio close," Matthew said.

"I will." Riley zipped up and headed out the back door to the chief's SUV. This was more like it, she thought, finding Tessa Barton's address in the GPS.

The main roads were clear but when she tried to turn left onto Tessa's street, the SUV's tires spun on the snow, and she was reminded that this was not Arizona. She knew however what it was like to drive in torrential rain and did the same here. A light foot on the gas and brakes to maintain control.

The two-story abode had a cottage feel with cheery yellow paint and white trim. Or maybe that was the snow framing the roof and windows. Bushes were mounds of white and the tree limbs were heavy with snow.

It was cold—too cold to snow, too cold to let the snow melt —and Riley wondered how long they would all be trapped in this pretty but frigid landscape.

She parked in the street as the driveway wasn't plowed. Smoke puffed from the chimney, adding a welcoming feel. Leaving the SUV, her boots crunched through a thin path of snow from the yard to the house that had dog prints. How sweet—Tessa must have a pet, and she'd made the dog its own little run. From the size of the prints, Riley would guess a medium-sized pup.

From the height of the gold in the snow, she'd say male.

The front door was painted pale blue. The porch had been shoveled just enough to make room for the dog and herself. The door opened as Riley reached the bottom step.

"Morning!" A woman in her late thirties, big hazel eyes, round face, and brown hair in a cute chin-length bob, greeted Riley with a bright smile. She held a steaming mug of coffee and had a gray-muzzled black terrier at her feet. Her smile turned to puzzlement. "Is there a problem?"

The uniform Riley wore had caused concern. "No! May I come in?"

"Sure."

The woman stepped back and the dog barked as if to alert her there was a stranger coming in.

"Muffin! I can see we have company," the woman said. "He's all bark and no bite. Back up, pup." She raised her head to Riley. "I'm Tessa Barton."

"Officer Riley Harper." Riley entered the warm and cozy home. "I tried calling but there was no answer."

"Oh! I probably have the ringer off. I always forget to turn it back on again."

A short man with dark-brown hair and glasses peeked his head out, holding a coffee pot with an oven mitt. "Everything all right?"

"I think so," Tessa said, gesturing toward the sofa where Muffin had taken his seat. A bag of yarn and knitting needles were on the side with the dog. Riley assumed that was Tessa's normal spot. "Officer Harper, this is Ethan Travis—he rents a room with me."

"Coffee?" Ethan asked, raising the pot.

"No, thank you," Riley said. "I won't take up much of your time." She followed Tessa into the living area. The fire added warmth and comfort.

Muffin watched her with dark canine eyes, just waiting for her to make one wrong move. Riley sat on the far side of the couch, her hands folded in her lap.

"How many rooms do you have for rent?" Riley asked once Tessa was settled. Muffin put his chin on Tessa's leg to watch Riley.

"Three downstairs. I have the upstairs suite for my private space. Shared kitchen and living room." Tessa patted Muffin's back. "I'm an aspiring thriller writer and I spend most of my time dreaming of getting published. Hence the ringer."

"A writer? Wow—good luck. We're all readers in my family."

"Thanks. I inherited the house from my husband. He passed away five years ago in a boating accident."

Instincts clicking in, Riley focused on what Tessa was saying. One dead man in this woman's life, and now another. She'd need to dig further.

"I'm sorry to hear that."

Tessa shrugged. "It was a long time ago. I learned to make do for myself—mostly. I like renting out the rooms, not only for the small income but also the company."

Riley nodded. The woman shared a smile as Ethan whistled in the kitchen, obviously at home.

"Did you used to rent a room to Lars Sorenson?"

Tessa's face clouded. "Yes, he was with us for a year or so. I prefer long-term residents. Helps knowing you have a steady income. Ethan moved from Portland to the island three years ago to work at the medical center. He's a nurse practitioner."

"Oh. That's great. Have you ever had a full house?"

"During the summer months I normally have all the rooms rented." Tessa frowned. "You asked about Lars?"

"Yes." Riley didn't add to the answer and waited for Tessa to fill the awkward void. The ploy worked.

"Lars left to take a job in Bangor," she said, her cheeks pink.

Ethan came out of the kitchen to the living room with the pot to top off Tessa's mug. "He stiffed Tessa. I told her she should file a claim and sue his ass, but she won't."

"Oh, Ethan. It's not a big deal."

"A couple grand would fix the back porch," he said, feeling free to share his opinion. Probably friends.

"Did you know Lars well?" she asked Ethan.

"Didn't like him. Sure you don't want a cup?" When Riley shook her head, Ethan returned to the kitchen.

"He's protective," Tessa said in a soft voice. "Always looking out for me."

"How was Lars when he lived here? Did he bother you at all?"

She glanced down at her clasped hands. "He was all flirty and fun when he first came here to live, then things changed. He was drinking night and day and in bad moods practically all the time."

"Were you frightened of him?"

"No, not really. Sometimes he'd come into the kitchen and talk. He liked my cooking." She chuckled. "Then he started telling me things that nobody else knows."

"Anything you can tell me."

She cleared her throat. "This was his story and I never wanted to share it with anybody. But I can see you're concerned." Tessa bit her bottom lip, and a few tears blurred her eyes. She leaned forward, speaking in a low voice, "I don't hate him and I'm not afraid of him either. I feel sorry for the man he became…but he really had no choice."

"I understand. Bad things happen to kids all the time, and once they become legal adults, the rest is up to them. Most of them can't turn the page or find happiness."

Tessa nodded. "That's him to a tee. He had a terrible start in life. Father not around, his mom a crack addict. He slept in a small room off the kitchen, and the place was so dirty he'd see rats running around when he went to bed at night. His mother rarely brought food home, just alcohol and snacks. When he was about six, he left her snoring on the ragged old couch, mouth open, a bottle in her hand."

"Was that the last time he saw his mother?"

"Yes, but he didn't know it at the time. He went two blocks to a corner store, then snuck a loaf of bread into a brown bag, peanut butter, and a small package of fried chicken before making a dash out the door. The police caught him, of course, and he was taken away from his mother, became a foster kid, moved from one home to another. He hated the world. Can you blame him?"

"I get it. My heart aches for all these young kids that were horribly mistreated, but it doesn't make what they do as adults acceptable. They have to live by the same code of ethics that the rest of us do."

Tessa had gotten up and was pacing nervously. Riley wondered just how close Tessa and Lars had been. Both had been consenting adults, but had her innocence been taken away too?

Lars had been a hound dog. No, Riley thought, looking at Muffin with his loyal posture, Lars would give dogs a bad name.

"When Lars left, did he tell you why he was leaving?"

"A managerial job with higher pay. He asked me to send his things along when he got a new apartment."

Cheeky. Lars seemed pretty certain the women in his life would do his bidding. Must have been a stud in the sack. "Did you?"

Tessa full-on blushed. "I did. He didn't have much." She scratched under Muffin's chin. "I heard from Valerie that Lars was in town. Kind of hoped he'd come by and pay back my money."

"That would have been the decent thing to do." Would this have made Tessa Barton angry enough to kill?

The woman seemed sweet, but appearances were often deceiving. Riley would look into Tessa's past and find out more about how her first husband had died.

Tessa sipped her coffee and put the mug back on the end table. "May I ask why you're here about Lars? What has he done now?"

Riley had to come up with something plausible. "We just have some questions for him. Please don't mention this to anyone, but Coby Jenkins had a break-in at his place." She watched as Tessa put two and two together.

"Oh, no." Tessa rubbed her arms. Muffin growled. "I've only met Coby a few times at the The Shack but from what Lars said, he really believes the best of people."

Riley saw that same trait in Tessa—unless the woman, a professional storyteller, was lying.

She got up. "If you see him…"

The light had gone from Tessa's face before she schooled her expression. The woman was either in love with Lars or had a soft spot for him.

Riley assumed Tessa Barton had been in love with her husband too. Her *dead* husband.

CHAPTER NINE

RILEY LEFT TESSA'S BOARDING HOUSE, ADDING NOTES TO BE checked later when she returned to the station. While it was interesting about dead Mr. Barton, the important thing was that Tessa hadn't seen or heard from Lars the night of his death. Snow was falling hard and fast, and she had no time to lose. Plugging the address for Kimber's house into the GPS, she feared not being able to connect. She let out a breath when the map appeared.

Kimber's home was two blocks from The Shack and had a brown wood frame on top and three feet of rock on the bottom. Small, sturdy, and built to weather the island storms. It was much more compact than Riley's rental home.

Smoke billowed from the stack on the roof, inviting and welcoming. Riley jumped out of the SUV, careful not to slip on the snow. The path from the door to the mailbox had been shoveled before, but at least six inches had accumulated since.

Riley gave a quick knock, and the door opened quickly.

"Hello!" Tamara, Kimber's best friend from college, stepped back into the foyer to let Riley in. Lars had hit on the pretty brunette at the birthday party, until Kimber told him to back off.

"Hi...I don't know if you remember me from the other night..."

"I do—first female officer in Sandpiper Bay," Tamara said with a grin. "Kimber's in the kitchen making us some soup." She tossed her head and her light-brown shoulder-length bob swirled like a commercial. "Kimber and I have been friends, like forever." She waved her hand. "Come on in."

Riley stomped on the welcome mat to clear her boots from snow, then followed Tamara down the hall. The bungalow had probably been built in the fifties, with narrow space between rooms which were ten by fourteen at most. In the living room was a couch and armchair and bright yarn on both seats. Riley recalled that they were crocheting blankets.

"Hey!" Kimber turned from the stove as they entered the kitchen. Savory spices scented the small area. "Officer Harper, what have I done?" Kimber teased. "You were so mysterious when you called wanting to talk. We only smoked a joint, maybe two. Right Tamara?"

Her friend shrugged and arched her brow. "You did. I prefer wine."

"So, there you have it." Kimber held up her hands. "You going to arrest me, or join us for lunch?"

"Do I have to make a choice?" Riley played along with them, but she had no intention of eating. She had too much to do.

"Why don't you sit down? I'm making ham and cheese sandwiches to go with bean soup." Kimber took a loaf of bread from the refrigerator, along with ham slices, cheese, and butter.

"Do you mind if I ask you a few questions in front of Tamara? Or would you prefer to answer them alone?" Riley darted Tamara a friendly smile, meaning no offense.

"Heck. There isn't anything about me that Tam doesn't know. You want a sandwich as well as the soup?"

"None for me, but thanks. I need to get back to the station. Are you prepared for the storm?"

"Yep. We get plenty of nor'easters. I don't have a generator, but we've got candles, the fireplace, and canned stuff. Lots of wine and lots of yarn." Kimber assembled a sandwich. "We're already starting on next year's Christmas gifts."

"Smart! I tried to knit but it was a lesson in frustration. I took up yoga instead." Riley removed her heavy police jacket, hanging it over the back of the chair, then sat at the round table. A window with gingham curtains, open to the snowfall, was behind her. "Where do people go that don't have supplies?"

Kimber focused on her task and didn't look up. "The library is usually open for folks in need of shelter. Are they saying it's going to be that bad?" She glanced at Riley in alarm.

Riley folded her hands on her lap. "This is my first storm. Matthew keeps saying it could wobble out to sea, but Trevor Dunfield, the paramedic?"

Kimber nodded.

"He offered a wager, thinking it will hit. Personally, Matthew and I are waiting to hear from Captain Wyatt, who has a sonar machine, to tell us. Just, well, be prepared. It sounds like you are."

"I'm sure the 'possible' storm warning isn't the only reason you stopped by," Kimber said with a wink. "What can I help you with?"

Tamara chose the seat closest to the stove and picked up the cup of tea she'd been drinking. She had pretty hands with slender fingers. No rings. "I'm curious, too."

"I'm just fact-finding at the moment. Lars Sorenson has been missing since the night of the birthday party. When did you see him last?"

Tamara and Kimber exchanged a look, then Kimber placed a sandwich in a sizzling pan with butter.

"I heard a rumor that he's not missing," Kimber said, "but in the morgue."

Riley laced her fingers together and maintained composure. "Where did you hear that?"

"I'm a bartender and people talk. I can't remember who said what. Is it true?" Kimber flipped the sandwich, which was a perfect golden brown.

Riley exhaled. "That information is confidential right now so I can't say yes or no. Matthew and I are conducting interviews to find out Lars's movements that day."

Sheesh. How many people around here knew about Lars? You couldn't get away with much on such a remote island. Riley hoped that the truth would prevail—sooner than later.

"Lars showed up at The Shack around two that afternoon," Kimber said. "Me and Valerie were working the bar, and Coby was in the kitchen. Lars was begging him for another chance. Coby's got a big heart and he felt sorry for Lars that he had nowhere to go—the jerk's own fault. The ferry was closed, as you already know."

Riley made a note of the time—it matched what Coby had told her. "Even though he and Coby'd had a previous altercation?"

"He's a saint. Coby asked Katie if he could bring Lars to the party, to keep an eye on him, I think." Kimber flipped a second sandwich. "Last I saw of Lars was when he was at the Lobster Pot. Not that I give a damn." Kimber had a hand on her hip as she turned to face Riley. She removed the soup from the heat and let it sit as she got out plates and bowls.

"I noticed hostility between you," Riley acknowledged with a brief smile. "How well did you know him? I'm aware that you worked together before he quit. Lars was handsome and charming in his bad-boy way. Although I only met him once, I could see he liked the ladies. Not that I'm suggesting..."

"We hooked up a time or two. It was no big deal—strictly sex with no expectations. I think he tried every interested female over sixteen in town." Kimber shrugged. "It's slim pickings around here, and girls on the island learn to share."

Riley hid her cringe as she typed into her phone. She would *not* let Kyra be humiliated like that...bonus to her contract falling through? Her daughter would be saved from a small dating pool. However, Kyra knew her self-worth so if Riley remained here, they'd manage until Kyra went to college where she'd meet plenty of decent, educated guys.

"I'm sorry to hear that," Riley said, also thinking of Emily. "It shouldn't be that way. Why don't more young women go to the mainland to work?"

"I can't speak for everyone, but it's a hard world off the island. I went to college with Tamara, graduated with a business degree, and got a job in a bank. Came home after the first year with a broken heart. I discovered my boyfriend was actually married." Kimber brought the dishes to the table. "He called me naïve. As if trusting him was *my* fault."

What a creep. Riley sighed. "I want to protect Kyra from the wolves. That wasn't your fault, Kimber."

"Kyra's a cutie!" Tamara interjected. "And I've told Kimber a thousand times that her ex was a predator in a three-piece suit."

Riley agreed. "Lars noticed Kyra, Kimber, and you told him to back off—you mentioned Emily?"

"Emily works at The Shack... Lars was really taking advantage of her innocence. Flirting, kissing in the back room." Kimber's nose scrunched. "I tried to give Emily a heads-up, but she ignored me. Said that I was jealous of true love. Poor sweetie. When Lars left, she moped for a month. I offered to talk with her, but she shut me out."

Riley added true love into her notes section. Lars had poorly used the females on Sandpiper Bay.

Kimber remained on a tangent. "Lars could be fun but a real ass too. Before he left, he took two hundred from my purse, and cash from the till. I heard that he broke into Coby's safe and helped himself. Karma is a bitch!"

He'd stiffed Tessa too. How many people had Lars burned before fleeing the island? Coming back and expecting to be welcomed was ludicrous. Did he have an ulterior plan? She thought of the guys he played cards with. Miguel claimed that Lars owed him money. What if Lars had come to collect a debt? She typed a note to ask Nelson.

"Do you know if Lars had a car?" Riley asked.

"Nope," Kimber answered. "He rode a bicycle when he used to live here last year. Cheap and easy to get around."

Tamara made room for the platter of sandwiches. "Kimber, when are you going to leave this place? I've told you over and over that you can stay with me."

"It's not going to happen," Kimber responded, taking her seat. "This is home."

Tamara looked irritated as she turned to Riley. "I live in Hartford, Connecticut. It's a great place, filled with job opportunities and men galore." She giggled as she handed out napkins. "I could have a date every second night if I chose. But I don't. I prefer to enjoy life and take things nice and slow. You could do that too, Kimber."

Kimber shrugged. "There's a man of interest right here," she muttered, getting up for cups and a pot of hot water for more tea. She placed them in the center of the table.

Tamara frowned. "He's not available, you know that."

Riley watched the best friends with interest. "Are you talking about Matthew? I saw you guys hit it off at the party. They don't get nicer than that."

"No." Kimber's face flamed. "The old cliché—I've fallen in love with my boss."

That was too bad for Kimber because Coby and Maria were crazy for each other. Riley steered away from the topic. "Is there anything else you two know about Lars and his shenanigans that might help with this investigation?"

"You keep using the word, 'investigation' and not search," Tamara said, her gaze on Riley. "You're looking for a suspect, aren't you? Someone with a reason to want him gone—gone, for good."

Without answering the question, she asked, "Tamara, you seem like an intelligent, sensible woman." Riley pictured her in the courtroom as a judge or a detective. "What's your line of work?"

"I'm a prosecutor in a big law firm." Tamara grinned. "But I suppose you already deduced that."

"I hoped you might be one of us, but you get paid a heck of a lot more." Riley smiled. "If you hear anything, give us a call?" She reached in her pocket and handed over her card.

Tamara took it. "I will—but we don't plan on leaving the house at all today."

Riley stood. "Thank you, ladies, for the friendly chat, and for letting me interrupt your lunch. Stay safe during the storm, if it doesn't wobble." She rolled her eyes at the silly word and shrugged back into her jacket.

Kimber walked her to the door. "It's nice to have you here in Sandpiper Bay, Officer. You are a great example that the job is about skill, not gender."

"That's very kind, Kimber."

Riley returned to the SUV with a lighter step and got inside. She turned on the engine and tapped into her notes. A wind gust rocked the SUV, reminding her that they were in a race against the storm.

Fact: Lars was a predator. Vigilantes sometimes took matters into their own hands when it came to protecting their families. If Lars had toyed with Emily's emotions, would Sam have gotten involved? Lindsay had seemed to know more about the situation. Maybe Emily had confided in her mother.

The time on the dash flashed one o'clock.

No cell service, so she radioed into the station. Rosita answered. "Hi Riley! Matthew had me come in to answer phones—he had a call out to the Washburne place. One of their kids, a fifteen-year-old boy who is friends with Ryker, claims that he and Ryker were supposed to meet up at the woods the night Lars went missing. Matthew's interviewing him now."

"Interesting." Riley wondered if Ryker also knew Lars or if this was coincidence.

"Matthew said you should drop by the ferry depot. Captain Wyatt is going to meet you there to show you the weather sonar. How are you doing? What's it like out there?"

"The sky is getting darker. I suppose this is normal?" Riley teased.

"Let's just say, I'm looking forward to hearing Wyatt's report." Rosita laughed. "We can go from there when you get to the station afterward."

"Thanks, Rosita. See you soon."

Riley drove by the house. Kyra and her mom were bundled up outside, playing in the snow—both seemed happy so she kept driving toward the depot. If the storm came, would this affect Kyra going to school on Tuesday?

She passed by the chicken man's house and glanced at the porch. It was empty, the rocking chair covered in snow. Ollie Pelletier was a local legend. Riley and her family had first seen him when they'd departed the ferry and were waiting for Chief Barnes to pick them up. The old man surveyed the depot from his throne, cooing to the chicken on his lap as one would a favorite pet.

Riley did a cautious U-turn and parked. Wyatt Michaud not only captained the ferry barge but manned the office. He had part-time help in the busy months.

The small building had a parking lot with room for a dozen

cars but only one was in the lot now. She exited and dashed toward the door.

Cripes! Her feet slid right out from under her, and she landed on her back. Snow had camouflaged the layer of ice beneath. Breathing heavily, Riley glanced up and down the road. No witnesses to her fall, which was a blessing to her pride. The wind had been knocked out of her, but thanks to the many layers she wore, she doubted she'd sustained any injuries other than being black and blue.

Taking deep breaths, she attempted to get up.

"Officer Harper? Riley—are you all right?" She peered upward as Captain Wyatt Michaud gazed down on her. His ruddy face was more flushed than normal, most likely due to the exertion of hurrying across the parking lot to her. His blue eyes had a bright glow under bushy white brows.

Riley attempted a smile. "Just the man I wanted to see. If you'll lend me your hand, we can speak in your office."

"Of course, Officer." Once she was on her feet, the captain offered his arm in a gallant gesture, and she quickly tucked hers under his. "Rosita called to say you'd be dropping by. Not literally," he chuckled.

Pride stinging, Riley hobbled to the door and ducked inside once Wyatt opened it. "Thanks. I'm curious to see your weather setup. Trevor Dunfield claims the storm will hit. Others aren't sure. Officer Sniders told me you have a sonar machine that will give us an accurate and updated view of the storm."

"Trevor has a seventy-forty success rate on his guesswork." Wyatt smacked his large palms together. "Let's have a look at the machine. I've been watching the systems converge all day."

Wyatt walked across the floor, boots squelching as the rubber soles met the tile. Riley's boots were a tad quieter but not much.

"That Matthew has made something of himself, I'm glad to see. Know his family real well." Wyatt scrubbed his jaw. "Come to think of it, everybody knows everybody; that's why I like small towns. Strangers stick out like a sore thumb."

"Captain, the weather?" She glanced down at the smart phone on her wrist, noting the time. "I have to get back to the station."

"It'll be up in a jiffy."

She scanned the office, but the only chair was his, behind the desk. "Wyatt, you told us at the party that Lars Sorenson had taken the last ferry Friday morning. What time was that?"

"Oh, uh, ten."

"Did he have a car?"

"No, ma'am." The captain sounded certain. Where had Lars gone between ten and two that day?

"Did you see Lars later?"

"Nope. He wasn't a good example of the male species that night, drunk and out of control." Wyatt turned to her. "How's Susan faring? Your mom and daughter are both strong females, just like you."

Riley liked that observation, a lot. If there was a nor'easter coming, then they'd need to be strong. "They're enjoying the novelty of snow."

Wyatt sat on the office chair and pulled up the screen. Her gaze had a hard time focusing on the swirls and bright colors.

"Your mother is a real fine lady. Doesn't belong to anyone, does she?" Wyatt tapped her wrist to get her attention.

Riley reluctantly turned her head from the dots and numbers. "Sorry, what did you say?"

"Your mother. If she's not seeing anyone, I'd like to take her to coffee or lunch. She mentioned that she likes to read. So do I. Dan Brown and James Patterson—before he got everybody writing for him. Did you ever read that Jason Bourne series? That was a good one."

Swallowing the adverse reaction of Susan dating Wyatt, Riley cleared her throat. "Mom's not seeing anyone, but you'd have to ask her. Now, back to the screen. What does all this mean?"

"Dear God!" His complexion turned bright red, and he pointed a shaking finger, leaning toward the colors and whirls.

"What? What's wrong?" Panic swept through every inch of her. What kind of danger had she brought her family into? She took a few deep breaths and listened intently to Captain Wyatt.

"Don't see this very often—Maine is hit by storms all winter long. Ya never get used to it." His blue eyes had sharpened like laser beams.

Riley's stomach knotted. "If that's supposed to be reassuring, it isn't."

"Sorry! See this mass here? It's an ice storm and it's coming our way tonight... It will collide with the blizzard predicted."

"What changed? What about the wobble out to sea?" Apprehension trickled down her spine. Bad guys you could toss in jail, but weather played by its own rules.

"Weather shifts on a dime—one day it's sunshine, the next it's rain. Keeps weathermen in jobs." Wyatt nodded smugly.

She leaned her hip to the table to face Wyatt. "Captain? I must know the worst. Do we need to alert the islanders?"

"I'll put out a broadcast on the radio. Tell people to prepare and stay inside. Tonight, we need to batten down the hatches." Wyatt jabbed his forefinger to the screen. "This mega storm will create widespread damage across the island. Power outages, trees downed. Roofs caved. One storm, we had boats from the marina in the center of the park... This is ten times more catastrophic. Things will be bleak for the next few days at least."

"I think I preferred the mild winter," she said, sounding much calmer than she felt. "Any chance it will miss us?"

"I wouldn't put money on it. This will up Trevor's accuracy average."

Riley fought back a stream of tears. This was no time to

break down; it was her job to remain calm in a crisis, to comfort others and restore confidence and hope.

Crap! Who was she kidding?

Captain Wyatt stood up and chucked a knuckle under her chin. "It'll be all right. Lived around here all my life, and I've seen plenty of disasters in my day, but we islanders always come through." He rubbed her arms and bent so they were eye to eye. "You'll see. You and your family just need to tuck in at the house. Center rooms, away from windows. You ever been in a hurricane?"

Riley shook her head, thinking of the second bedroom downstairs that they were using as storage. It could be cleared out and they could make it comfortable for the night. "I need to make some calls." She breathed deeply. "Being the new kid on the block, besides the radio, is there another way to get the message out? Do you have an alarm to let people know if a big storm is on its way?"

"The fire station has a special siren to alert the townsfolk for this type of emergency. People will know what to do." While she was still wrapping her mind around this, Wyatt asked, "Can I give you some advice?"

She gulped. "Sure."

"The aftermath of the storm will leave the island a mess and it will be hard work with all hands needed on deck. Folks know to stay inside their homes until its over—no emergency services, including ambulance and police, will be out patrolling. This is the time, Officer, for you to prepare your community, and then go home and protect your family."

"Thank you," she answered in a shaky voice. She gave him a brief smile and then left. The sky was charcoal with the white of the snow in contrast.

Standing outside the chief's car, Riley held up her cell phone to see if she could get signal to the mainland. Two bars. Yes!

She dialed his number, not daring to risk losing the connection by getting inside the SUV. Barnes answered right away.

"Harper? What's going on?"

Riley told him about the approaching ice storm crashing into the blizzard and quickly updated him on where they stood in the investigation. More questions, less answers. He muttered a few curses, then told her he might try to fly in that night on the small seaplane airstrip on the opposite side of the island.

"You might be better to stay where you are, Chief. Getting to the island during a storm doesn't make sense. You'd be risking your life and the pilot's. Wait until tomorrow or the next day." She swallowed and added, "Think of your family. Matthew, Rosita, and I can take care of things for now."

He grunted. Stewed. She imagined him pacing and glaring at the phone. At last, he said, "Fine. I don't like it, but Shelley's staring at me and threatening to hide the keys."

Riley gave a wry chuckle. "Have you been in touch with Dr. Lakshmi?"

"Still nothing. She told me she's as busy as a one-armed paper hanger. When I was obviously surprised at her word choice, she shared that she'd learned it from Serge. She'll let me know as soon as possible. You hunker down now, hear? And tell Matthew and Rosita, keep their radios on and nobody be stupid. We don't want heroes, got it?"

"I will relay the messages," Riley promised. "Bye."

Riley had the car door open when she heard awful screeching noises coming from Ollie's house. She slammed the door shut, pocketed her phone, and ran up his stairs—sliding on the slick steps. Knocking on his door, she heard some kind of commotion going on inside. She pounded on the door. "Ollie, are you okay?"

Ollie swore loudly, then shouted back, "Go away. I'm fine. Cooking myself dinner for tonight."

The chicken! The sound of squawking and cursing continued for a few more seconds. What could she do?

She nudged the door with her arm and it opened a crack. Peeking inside she saw Ollie with a butcher knife in his hand, chasing his pet chicken.

Riley felt tears sting her eyes. Should she draw her weapon and burst through the door?

Her job was to save lives—but did that include another poor plump chicken?

CHAPTER TEN

RILEY'S BODY WAS TENSE, BUT SHE MANAGED TO REACH THE station without careening the SUV off the road. Streetlamps were clouded by snow flurries. The winds were definitely picking up and it looked like seven at night instead of almost two in the afternoon.

She parked behind the station and went in through the breakroom, where Matthew pored over his notes—printed papers were strewn across the table. Riley could hear Rosita on the phone at the front desk where Nancy usually sat.

"Hey!"

Matthew whirled. "Oh! You scared me. Do you realize that Ryker and this Washburne kid, Dorian, were tailing Lars before he left the island?"

"Months ago?" Riley unzipped her jacket, glad to be warm. "How could I know that?"

"Right." Matthew stood up. "Want me to make another pot of coffee? I could use a hit of caffeine."

"Yeah. That would great." She took her coat off completely and stacked it with her gloves on an end chair. "So. Why were they doing that?"

"I guess Ryker didn't think Lars should be flirting with his sister." Matthew shrugged.

Riley crossed her arms and leaned against the counter. "Did Ryker and Dorian ever catch up to Lars?"

"He said that they hadn't." Matthew pressed the start button on the old coffeemaker. "What did you learn?"

"Lars stiffed Tessa Barton a few months' rent when he left."

"What a loser!"

"Worse is that Tessa had a soft spot for the man. And Kimber said that Emily fancied herself in love with Lars too."

"I don't understand why girls go for the guys that suck." His cheeks were pink with emotion. Was he thinking of the woman he'd almost married?

"Me either," Riley said. Kimber and Matthew were both bound to Sandpiper Bay. Maybe when this was all over, she could play matchmaker. "Did you ever catch up with Bernie?"

"I swung by the marina on the way back from the Washburnes but they were in full boat storage mode to get the ships and watercraft tied up. Not the right time."

"Getting answers is rarely a straight line," she commiserated.

Rosita hurried back to the kitchen. "Oh, is that coffee I smell? Hurray. What did people do before java juice?" She reached for three mugs from the cupboard and passed them out. "The phones are ringing off the hook. Radio too. People are getting scared about the upcoming storm. Wyatt put out a bulletin on the radio, saying it's going to be a big one. Ice, wind, snow. Catastrophe."

Riley nodded. "That's what he told me too. He showed me the sonar machine, which is out of this world. We need to prepare and then hunker down."

The three stared at the pot as it dripped.

"What else did you discover at Kimber's?" Matthew asked.

"She'd heard that Lars is dead while working at the bar but not who said it. I didn't confirm or deny."

"Sandpiper Bay's unique brand of communication. A whisper here, a murmur there." Matthew returned to his chair with his empty mug rather than stare at the machine. "Gossip thrives. Someone *must* know something."

"We can add to the board that Wyatt said Lars arrived at ten Friday morning, without a car. Kimber saw Lars at The Shack at three," Riley said. "Coby felt sorry about Lars being stranded on the island. Hey, Matthew, did Coby say whether or not Lars had a suitcase?"

"I was busy with Dorian and didn't get to it yet," Matthew said. The coffee finished brewing and Rosita topped off their mugs. Riley inhaled and the scent of dark brew jolted through her. She dared a hot drink. "Just what I needed."

Rosita blew and sipped, her eyes closed. "Agreed." She opened them and studied the board. "You've collected a lot of information. Is there anything you'll be able to do before tonight's storm?"

"Let me think." Matt ran a hand through his ginger hair. "The doctor thread is on hold because Dr. Lakshmi is not only waiting for Lars to unthaw but helping patients."

Riley took another drink. "Rosita, if you have time, will you look up Tessa Barton? Her husband died several years ago, and she inherited the house. I'd like to know how he died, and if it was on the up and up."

"Oh," Rosita said. "A black widow."

Matthew shivered. "I hate spiders."

Riley and Rosita didn't explain that it was also a term for a woman who killed her mates. "She seems like a kind person, but if she was also in love with Lars, and he duped her, well …it's worth crossing off the list."

Rosita cupped her mug. "You got it. Anything else?"

"We need to ask Ryker why he was stalking Lars with his friend Dorian and didn't mention it," Matthew said. "Dorian said he didn't know."

He squinted at the whiteboard and Riley added Dorian to the person of interest list with a marker.

"I'd love to talk with Emily about her feelings for Lars," Riley said, "but I doubt her family will let me close without a good reason. Maybe we should just drop by, Matthew, and make a neighborly call."

Matthew's eyes closed partially as he finished his cup of joe.

It had been a busy day, emotionally exhausting, with her family in the rental all alone, and some crazed killer running loose. Not that they knew that. And now there was a storm too. She wanted to go home, sit in front of the fire, have dinner and a big glass of wine, before a night of backgammon or Monopoly. *Not going to happen, Harper.*

The phone rang and Rosita refilled her mug before taking it to the front desk. "I'm coming!"

Matthew slumped in his chair. He was as exhausted as she was, yet they still had so much more to do.

"How late should we stay open tonight?" The station was usually closed at four on the weekends, with the number to call for emergencies posted on the door and listed in the answering message. Riley blew out a breath and tapped the pen to her coffee cup.

"It's as dark as midnight out there already," Matthew murmured. "We can't look for physical clues outside, regarding Lars. We really just need to get the community prepared for the storm. I hate to say it, but we should shift gears."

Just then, Rosita rushed back, her dark eyes flashing, chest heaving.

"What is it? Has something happened?" Riley took a step in her direction.

Rosita nodded. "That was Katie. Lobster Pot Katie." She panted. "Her brother Don wants to speak with the two of you about something that might pertain to the missing person you mentioned earlier—he's not sure."

They glanced at each other. "Thanks, Rosita. We've got this." Matthew patted her arm.

"You think it might be a break in the case?" Rosita flushed. "How exciting."

"Could be, or could be nothing," Riley answered. "Investigations are difficult. You hear from people all the time eager to help, and we take every call seriously. Most don't pan out, but once in a while you find a gem—something that had gone unnoticed or dismissed as not being important." She rubbed her hands together. "Glad you answered that call, Rosita."

Matthew already had his jacket on and was holding hers.

"Guess we're not having an early night after all." Riley shrugged her coat on and grabbed her gloves. "I'll let my mom know that we'll be a few extra hours. You driving?"

"Yup. With any luck we'll get a breakthrough in this case and leave with some of her clam chowder to take home."

They left Rosita manning the fort and headed out in the cold.

Settled in the car, Riley thought about Don. Had it only been this morning when he'd helped her with the generator, and she'd given him her phone number? Why had he not mentioned seeing anything then?

"Let's hope Don has something to help us track Lars, and add another tack to the timeline," Matthew said.

"Agreed." Riley stared out at the falling snow. "We need to nail down where Lars went after Coby's place. His manager, Valerie, closed The Shack at midnight, and I'm sure Lars wouldn't have dared to show his face there after stealing from Coby." Riley was silent for a moment, attempting to put the scattered pieces together.

"What are you thinking?" Matthew shot her a quick glance before returning his concentration to the road. "I can hear the wheels churning inside your head."

"Lars returns after five months gone and no one wants to

put him up, so kindhearted Coby agrees to let him stay for one night only. Why steal from his benefactor at midnight and then dart off into the wind and snowfall? Couldn't he have cracked open the safe in the wee hours of the morning after a good night's rest?"

Matthew chuckled. "We're not dealing with someone who had a full deck."

Deck. Riley straightened. "You think he bolted from Coby's with the cash and headed to the shanties to pick up a game?"

"That sounds reasonable. Maybe too reasonable. Who knows what was going on in that warped head of his?"

Riley shivered. Even with the heat on she was chilled to the bone.

"Let's hope Don can enlighten us." Matthew's stomach growled and he hit it with a fist to quiet it down. "Let's hope Katie offers us leftovers."

She laughed, realizing that she hadn't eaten since breakfast. "My stomach is grumbling too, and my mouth is watering just hearing those words."

Before they reached the Lobster Pot, Riley used the radio to call her mother. Kyra answered, sounding perky and excited. "Mom! When are you going to be home? The weather channel says we're going to get the biggest nor'easter of the season!"

And here she'd feared Kyra would be frightened. "That's what folks are saying. We are going to be fine, though. Listen, Captain Wyatt suggested that we stay in a room without windows tonight because of the high winds. Can you and Nana set the storage room up with blankets and water? Snacks?"

"Okay." Kyra's tone lost some of its excitement.

"I'm not sure when I'll be home just yet, but you can use this radio to reach us in the car or at the station."

They said goodbye.

Matthew pulled up in front of a cabin next door to the Lobster Pot on the bay, and they got out. Riley knocked. A dog howled and a chain rattled. "Feeling like Ebenezer Scrooge right now," she said with a laugh. "With all the rattling chains."

"Spooky!" Matthew agreed. In the minute they'd been outside, snow had already collected on his cap. "That scene with the ghost always creeps me out."

"Who is it?" Katie called from the other side.

Carter opened the door. "Our favorite police officers, Katie my love." He waited for them to stomp their boots and brush off the snow before ushering them inside. He kept a firm grip on their German shepherd's collar.

Katie grinned. "Hey! I know you're here to speak with my brother, but we hope you can you stay for a taste of my stew?"

Don came out of a back room. "Hey, guys. Thanks for coming so soon."

Matthew stepped forward. "No prob. You called the station?"

"Katie did." Don reached for his coat on the tree by the door. "I'm not sure if this will help or not, but I got to talking with Katie and Carter and they suggested I tell you about it."

"What happened?" Riley smiled encouragingly. "Big or small, any information…"

"Shep barking woke me up out of sound sleep so I went to the back porch to check it out, but it was snowing really hard, and I didn't hear anything. I thought I smelled cigarettes," Don explained. He shoved his hands in his jean pockets.

"None of us smoke," Katie said, her blue eyes bright.

Riley nodded and shared a look with Matthew. Lars *did* smoke. This could help them find out where he'd gone after Coby's.

"What time?" Riley asked.

Don shook his head. "I didn't think to check."

Darn it.

Matthew said, "Lars Sorenson hasn't been seen since Friday night. We're investigating his whereabouts."

All three nodded—this obviously wasn't news.

"Did you take a look outside?" Riley asked.

"Not then. As I said, it was snowing." Don put on his coat. "It wasn't until I was out walking the dog, 'bout an hour ago, that I found a cigarette butt."

"Did you leave it there?" Matthew asked. Riley was already patting her pockets for an evidence bag.

Don nodded. "Sure did. I'll show you." He turned toward his sister. "We'll be back in a minute, Katie."

Riley didn't have to be asked twice. She headed for the back door that led to a deck with a panoramic view of the bay.

"Lars had a cigarette above his ear the night of the party," Riley said. "We know he smokes."

"You notice everything," Matthew mumbled.

"When you've been on the force as long as I have, you will too."

"This way." Don gestured to where he'd found the butt. "We can follow the path that Shep's made through the snow."

About fifty yards out they reached trees clustered on the edge of the property. Water lapped at a rocky beach. Was it possible to walk around the entire island?

"Here it is," Don said.

Matthew beat her to it and used a pair of tweezers to show the butt to Riley. "Check this out!"

It had a gold filter, just like the one Lars had. Excitement tingled her nape. "That's exactly the same. It's fancy." Riley moved her foot over the ground around the tree base where the butt had been. Lars had been stuck on the island by the storm. Why had he returned to Sandpiper Bay?

"Holy crap! Look at this," Matthew's voice hiked up like it usually did when he was excited.

Don bent over, looking closely but not touching.

Riley rounded the large pine and dropped to her knees. Silver and black. Cell phone size. Could it be? She pushed the snow away and sighed with frustration. The device was smashed and completely crushed. Had Lars done this, or had his killer?

Matthew drew out another evidence bag and used plastic gloves to place the cell phone inside. "Thanks for calling us, Don. This is mighty helpful."

"Can it be repaired?" Don asked.

"It's amazing what forensics does with these things," Riley said, getting to her feet. Don steadied her with a hand on her back. She smiled in thanks. "We should mark this with ribbon, Matthew, in case we need to come back here."

While he did that, Riley took pictures of the scene. The undisturbed snow was about four feet but in the protection of the trees, it was less than two. She imagined Lars running out of Coby's house into a storm. Would he just hang out here and smoke? Was he trying to form a plan?

She turned around to her partner. "Matthew, do these trees connect to Mackabee Woods?"

He considered. "The island isn't that big—everything connects."

Don stomped his feet, his cheeks red from cold. "Should we get back? Katie's stew will warm us all up again."

Riley and Matthew followed Don inside, but Riley's thoughts weren't on food. She was wondering how to fix the destroyed phone.

Katie gave them a warm welcome. "Go wash up, you guys, and I'll start serving when you're seated."

Matthew tugged at his scarf and gloves, then took off his jacket. The evidence bags were in his inner pockets.

Katie gestured for Riley to follow suit. "You do the same, Riley. There's a guest bathroom down the hall. And we have plenty of stew."

Don reached for Riley's coat as soon as she chucked it off. He smelled like expensive cologne.

Get a grip, Harper, she berated herself, admiring his shoulders as he hung her coat on a hook. Don turned and saw her watching him. He grinned. "Need any help finding that guest bathroom?"

She shook her head at his teasing tone. "Nope. Thanks again for showing us what you found." As attractive as he was, she and Matthew were officially on duty.

"Of course," Don said, backing up with raised hands.

Riley needed to be careful about sending out signals. With her family here and the one-year contract, Riley wasn't really available in a meaningful way.

Riley entered the dining room next to the kitchen, her mouth watering at the rich scent of Katie's beef and onion stew. She took the chair next to Matthew that had a view of the kitchen. Don removed a loaf of bread from the oven and sat it down on a wooden cutting board to cool. He appeared next to her with a crock of butter for the table and gave her a nudge and a sly wink. Her heart raced. She hadn't flirted with anyone in over a decade and didn't want to start now.

They all sat down, and Matthew filled them in about the ice storm colliding with the blizzard, which hadn't gone out to sea. They discussed what needed to be done, and how they could help their neighbors. Matthew said that the library would be open to offer shelter. He'd radioed the head librarian and it was all set up. The mayor was out of town for the long weekend, but the woman had supplies and had been through this before.

Riley listened to the conversation but ate her stew in silence. The phone. What clues might it hold? Who had Lars talked to? Why had he returned? There hadn't been any visible footprints because of the new snow.

"Rosita has been letting folks know...and Wyatt has broadcasted on the radio. This is supposed to be a mega storm. Will you help get the word out?" Matthew asked.

"I'll relay the message to Joan Higgins." Katie tapped her

soup spoon on the tablecloth. "That will be faster than any other means."

They all shared a laugh.

"That's a great idea." Matthew returned to his stew, eating quickly to finish his bowl.

When the meal was over—late lunch, early dinner, or hearty snack, who cared? It was amazing—Riley could think clearly again. She hated to bring up the case, but it was the reason they'd stopped by. "So. Lars Sorenson. What do you know of him?"

Carter put down his fork and leaned back in his chair. "The night of the birthday party, his behavior was disgusting. Katie and I wanted to throw him out but for Coby's sake we said nothing. Can't believe that Coby thought he was a changed man." He glanced at Riley, then Matthew. "My waiter told me that Lars wanted something stronger than alcohol, and if he could hook him up."

Riley wiped her mouth with her paper napkin. Their hands were tied on sharing the truth with their friends.

"Tell them everything, hon." Katie swiped crumbs into her empty bowl, then met their gazes. "Carter heard down at the marina that Lars was dead and found in a snowbank."

Riley nudged Matthew next to her. "Can you please do the department a favor and not pass this on?" she said. Frustration simmered but she tampered it down. Perhaps it was unrealistic to keep it under wraps.

"It's true, then?" Katie queried.

Matthew nodded glumly at his dish. "We can't tell you more than that."

"*You* didn't tell us anything." Katie smirked.

"You know what I mean!" Matthew said, flustered. "We can't confirm or deny."

"Who told you that, Carter?" Riley asked.

Carter shrugged. "Murphy's Marina is where everyone goes for supplies, so it's a natural hub for gossip."

"I see." Riley figured she might make a stop there when, God willing, she visited the Hamilton kids next. "We can't give information on the investigation but we're very thankful, Don, that you alerted us."

"A killer on the island and us all trapped." Katie giggled nervously. "Sounds like a movie or a Sandra Brown novel."

Don patted her hand. "This might not be fiction, but I promise you that nobody would harm a hair on you or Carter's head. They'd miss your dinners too much."

Katie attempted a smile, but she still had a worried look.

Shep whined and Carter scratched the dog's ears. "Everyone will be fine." He spoke optimistically. "We've got the best protection around with Shep on guard. Nobody will mess with us."

Riley nodded. Both the cigarette and the broken phone had been outside the boundary of their yard.

Katie straightened. "Lars came to eat at the Lobster Pot a few times, but we weren't friends. I've heard from reliable sources that Lars was a womanizer. Maybe he pissed off one of the ladies. A woman scorned. Might be the reason he fled so quickly all those months ago. But why would he return? He must have had a good reason."

From the way that Lars was killed, Riley could imagine rage or jealousy as a motive, but it would be difficult for a lone woman to manage the body. And the fingerprints around his neck had been large. The likeable Hamiltons came to mind. But which one?

"He made a mistake." Matthew shook his head.

On that depressing note, Riley stood before her partner ended up telling them everything. "Thanks for the great meal, Katie. And Don, we appreciate the tip. Matthew and I have a lot to do before dark and better get going. You all stay safe and keep tuned in to the radio."

Matthew clapped them all on the back. "We have a bunch of resilient people on this piece of rock, I'm proud to say. Stay close, stay in, and in the morning, we'll see what damage is done."

The two officers headed for the door.

"You be careful, too," Don said. He spoke to them both, but his gaze lingered on Riley.

Riley knew that sometimes, well, things just went to hell and all you could do was hold on and pray for another day.

CHAPTER ELEVEN

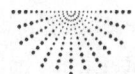

"Don likes you," Matthew said once they were in his sedan and driving toward the main road. It was slow-going in the dark. The streetlamps were coated with snow, giving little illumination for anyone on the streets this late afternoon.

"What? Are you thirteen?" Riley asked. "Now is not the time, Officer Sniders."

"Ooh. Does stress make you testy? My mom's that way."

"Hey!" Riley shifted on the seat wishing she could slow the snow to a reasonable speed so they could see out the windshield. There would be no clue-finding in this weather. "I think we should skip the marina for tonight and tackle it tomorrow. What do you say?"

"I was going to suggest it, but I didn't want you to think I was trying to bail. We aren't going to get anything accomplished in this mess."

"All right." Riley exhaled and let the list of things to do go. "The station then. We can send Rosita home. I'll take the SUV to my place. Where are you going to be tonight?"

"Family matters, as you know, and that's where I'll be. My parents have a five-bedroom house made of cement blocks and hurricane glass. My sisters are both out of town, or they'd be there with their brood." He glanced at her. "Will you be all right on your own? Maybe you should invite Coby and Maria and Dante to join you tonight."

"I told Mom to call Maria and ask. But the three wanted to stay home, and if things got rough, they'd call the fire department two blocks down."

"Suppose they'll be safe enough, but neither of their homes could stand up to a nor'easter if it's as bad as the last one. They'd be better going to the station, Maria's lasagna in hand, and bunk in for the night."

"I thought we only had two volunteers. Won't they be home with their families?"

"We have a retired chief still on the island. He lives alone. Bet my bottom dollar that he'll be manning the place tonight. The volunteers are likely on call, though nobody goes out during the worst of any storm."

Riley sighed, thinking about the night ahead. Three women who'd never faced anything so major before. So many things could go wrong, and probably would. Would it be rude to see if Matthew would leave his parents to stay with them? She'd never live it down. "Wouldn't mind doing that myself. It sounds comforting."

"Hey. You're one of the toughest people I know, but if you really mean it, I know Ma and Pop would welcome you and your family." Matthew slowed as the car started to slide when they turned into the station's back parking area.

"Really?"

"Yeah. The rooms are already made up because of the girls. Let me call them to make sure but I know they'll say yes."

"I might take you up on that offer, then. When I get home, I'll deliver the bad news and explain that this is not a normal storm —the last mega storm was nearly twenty years ago." She bit her lip. "I'll mention that during the last one, boats were overturned and floating down Main Street like it was a river. Power lines down, trees scattered on roads and people's lawn."

"How do you know that?"

"I was making it up. Don't tell me this happened?"

"And worse. Back then we weren't prepared for such an event. Now we're in better shape."

"That's a relief." How was she to tell her family? They'd sacrificed so much to come here with her and now they were in danger.

"Come over to our place. You'll be fine."

Riley dropped her head and closed her eyes. Said a silent prayer.

"Riley?"

"I'm fine. I'll let them know that we have options, but once it hits, the options are gone. We'll have to ride out the storm together."

"Which would be extremely brave, but not very smart."

"I'm not feeling that brave right now. Not for one second did I imagine that coming here could be dangerous. Two murders, two storms back-to-back." She gritted her teeth. "Kyra was right. We should have stayed home and faced our fears there; at least we could see them coming."

"Riley, take a deep breath. This too will pass." He used his arm to bump her elbow. "You've livened up the place, that's for sure. All we ever got to see around here is dead fish and arguments about who had the biggest one. Now—nothing but trouble. You need to slow it down a bit," he said with a cheeky grin.

She laughed. "Glad I could help."

"So, it's a deal then. Ma and Pop would kick my ass if I left you three alone."

"Matthew, this is so kind of you."

When they reached the station, Matthew said, "Seriously. It's not a good idea to face this alone."

The pair hurried inside through the back entrance and

entered the kitchen. Rosita had everything cleaned and put away.

"I should get going. My boyfriend's family is putting us up for the night and they've got a brick house with a generator. I talked to Nancy earlier, and she and her sister are together, also in a safe home. Darren is snug in the lighthouse. The librarian is on radio. I'm going to drop off some blankets from our store-room, all right?"

Matthew nodded. "Sure."

"Be safe, Rosita. We'll talk tomorrow." Riley opened the back door for her, and she and Matthew helped load Rosita's Jeep.

Back inside, he scrawled an address on a piece of scrap paper. "This is Ma and Pop's. If the GPS doesn't work, just follow Main to Anchor Lane and go left a block. It'll be the blue two-story house on the right."

"I don't know for sure," Riley said, "but probably." They did a last walk through the station to ensure they hadn't forgotten anything, then left from the back.

Matthew gave her a mock salute. "Keep in touch."

"I will, and thanks."

The drive home took all of her concentration. As she made the turn into their long driveway, the SUV's chained tires dug in for traction—the downhill trip made easy. Riley parked in the garage around back, noticing a path had been shoveled to clear her way.

She dug her keys out from deep inside her jacket and slid it in the lock. Stepping into the mudroom she removed her boots and bulky jacket, hearing music and laughter coming from inside her home. She hurried to join the two people she loved most in the world.

"Hey there. It sounds like a party!"

"It's a mega storm party. And we have all the lanterns and batteries ready." Kyra seemed happy. She didn't know to feel danger; her innocence came from excitement, not fear. If only Riley could keep her that way for the next twenty-four hours.

The radio was playing a dancing song about having a good time tonight. It wiped the smile from her face as she stood there watching them.

"What's wrong, Riley?" her mother asked. "You seem in a daze, and you're frightening me."

She shook her head, putting on a brave front. "I'm okay."

"Mom?" Kyra stopped dancing.

Shaking her head, she forced a laugh. "It's been a tough day that's all. Coming in and hearing music and the joy of laughter, well, it stunned me for a few seconds. Like a child's first visit to Disney World. Extraordinary. Magical."

"It's only a radio, Mom."

Susan clicked her teeth. "What you need right now is a good strong drink." She picked up and waved a bottle of bourbon that had been sitting on their kitchen counter. "That radio was not all we found in the garage!"

"Hold that thought, Mom. I'm going to shower and clean up first, but while I'm gone, I want the two of you to discuss a choice we have to make for tonight. Pros: Matthew has invited us to stay with his family. He genuinely wants us to come. We'd be surrounded by caring people, and not all alone."

Riley put her hands on her daughter's shoulders, looking her eye to eye. "Cons: We stay here and face a monster storm, one like nothing we've ever seen before."

Kyra's faced paled. "Does it get that bad?"

"I've heard it gets worse."

Without taking any more questions she dashed upstairs, showered, and dressed in jeans, a warm sweater, and thick socks.

Padding downstairs, she noticed her mom putting all the house decor away, removing anything close to the windows, placing a bunch of towels to block the doors. Prepping for the nor'easter. Looked like they were staying.

"Where's Kyra?" She helped her mom put items in the small closet, then reached for packing tape to secure the kitchen drawers. She hoped it would save their table plates, mugs and glasses, and the more delicate dishes that Susan had brought with her.

"In her bedroom packing." Susan was dragging the stand-up lamp next to the reading chair to lay it in a safer place.

Riley felt a jolt inside her. Did that mean…

"Matthew's place was a godsend. Didn't take us more than two minutes to figure that one out." She grinned and pushed her gray hair off her cheek. "Us Phoenix people are not used to catastrophes. We wouldn't cope very well. Not ashamed to say it, either."

"I'll give Matt a call to say we're coming—I've got the chief's SUV."

"Whatever you think, my dear. But if you're driving, then I'm drinking!"

ALL PACKED UP, SUV loaded, Riley turned the key. No sound. She tried a second time, and it coughed a little. Third time was lucky. The drive up the hill wasn't too difficult since she simply followed her tracks through the three to four feet of snow back up the way she'd come. The evergreens towered over the house and property, and she prayed they'd keep the home safe.

Fifteen minutes later, Riley and her family found a parking space under a carport. They hurried out along the shoveled path to the front door, and Riley knocked. Kyra huddled at her back, followed by Susan. It was opened by an older man with a small band of gray hair, bright-brown eyes, and a welcoming smile. "Come in, come in, you'll catch pneumonia standing out there."

He took hold of the two bags they'd packed and put them next to the door. "I'm Alfred, but around here they call me Alf. With an *A* not an *E*."

Susan chuckled at his joke. Riley introduced them all. They were shaking hands when a plump redheaded woman arrived. "Well now, who is this?" She peered at the three of them in the entrance and wagged her finger at Riley. "You must be the one Matthew is always talking about; he thinks you're the moon and the stars." Her eyes twinkled. "Welcome, Riley, and your mom and daughter."

"Thank you for having us at the last minute," Riley began, her hand out.

Instead of shaking hands, the woman swept her into an embrace. "About time we met. I'm Martha—like the vineyard."

Alfred proudly told his wife their names, and Martha, like the vineyard, showed them to the kitchen.

"Where's Matthew?" Riley asked.

"He stopped at the fire station to speak with the chief. Should be here any minute now." The front door slammed, and Martha smiled. "Looks like Matty's home."

Riley, Kyra, and Susan all turned at once.

Matthew's ginger hair was damp, and he ruffled it dry. "Hey, you got here okay! My folks treating you all right?"

Martha huffed. "No. I've had them washing the floors and polishing the silver."

Alf laughed and smirked at his son. "Then Mom asked Kyra here to pluck a turkey for dinner."

Matthew rolled his eyes.

"Which reminds me," Susan interjected, to get Matthew off the hot seat, "I brought a frozen lasagna and a bottle of bourbon I found stashed in the garage. Let me go…"

"I'm on it," Matthew looked at Riley. "Want to come with?"

Did that mean he had something to share with her about the case? "Sure." Riley left her family, stepping toward him.

"Come with? What's that supposed to mean?" Alfred wiped a hand over his mostly bald head. "You young people don't know how to talk proper English, or write in script either." He tsked. "Yet you all major in those dang tablets you have."

"Mine's a police radio, Pop." Matthew showed him the device the same size as a cell phone.

Kyra took her mobile out of her pocket. "Mine's for texting and for games."

Martha tugged Susan's wrist. "You ready for a drink?"

"It's only quarter past five," Alfred protested, checking his brown leather watch.

Riley watched the banter with amusement. Her mother was a fan of the five o'clock somewhere timeline.

"Never bothered me before," Martha answered—her mother's twin.

Riley hoped that the two moms would become friends. Susan never complained about being lonely, but she used to have a book group and social activities that she'd put to the side to join them in Sandpiper Bay.

"I'll take one when I get back," Riley said. They were certainly in for the night, which meant she wouldn't be violating her contract by a drink. She followed Matthew out the door.

Matthew laughed hard—once the front door was shut tight and there was no chance of being heard. Snow fell around them on the porch. She was glad she hadn't had time to take her coat off yet.

"So whatcha think?" Matthew gestured toward the house. "They're a little loony, but sweet as pie."

Riley unlocked the chief's SUV and Matthew raised the back hatch to gather the suitcases while she collected the bags. "I think your parents are adorable; even their jokes are funny." She gave him an appraising glance, seeing where he'd learned his humor and values. "You're fortunate to be so close to your family." She tucked the bottle of bourbon into the open carry-on. "Is there a reason that you wanted my help? Anything to do with the case?"

Matthew lowered his voice. "I stopped by Coby's on my way to the fire station, but he wasn't there. He's probably at Maria's with Dante. Did you discover anything, before we go inside and can't talk about Lars's death?"

"No." Matthew was so thoughtful it was almost unreal. "There's more to you than meets the eye."

"Nope. What you see is what you get." Matthew closed the hatch and they rushed back. Riley opened the door for him as he brushed by with the luggage.

The next ten minutes were taken up with getting settled into one of Matthew's sisters' rooms, which had been redecorated with blues and beiges rather than the hot pink of their youth, according to Martha. The house was a cozy *home*.

Riley had just been handed a bourbon and cola by the fireplace, next to her mom, and Kyra, drinking hot cocoa, when a knock sounded on the front door.

Who on earth?

Alf opened it wide, greeting a middle-aged couple with overnight bags. "Our neighbors," he explained.

"Thanks for inviting us," the woman said to Martha, who was shoulder to shoulder with Alf. "We hate being alone when things get crazy."

"Of course. We have three more guests!" Marsha ushered them in past the foyer while Alf shut the door, blocking the cold. "Officer Riley Harper works with Matty at the station. The cutie with the braids is her daughter, Kyra, and Susan, next to her—Riley's mother. They moved here this summer."

"I'm Winston." He gave them a nod. He had dark-brown hair, a mustache, and was short and stocky, wearing jeans and a Patriots cap. "My wife is Gloria."

Gloria offered her hand to them with a warm, welcoming smile in a round face. "So nice to meet you."

Alf poured the drinks, and Martha replenished a large cheese platter for the coffee table. For the first time in days, Riley allowed herself to relax. There was nothing she or Matthew could do to further the investigation. Lars was dead. His killer would be caught and brought to justice. Just not tonight.

After a generous meal, the family brought out Uno, a multi-player card game. The wind roared outside the windows, banging the shutters and a tree branch on the roof. The game was meant to distract them all from the weather, but it wasn't working.

Kyra sat so close to Riley they were practically attached at the hip.

Gloria gave a nervous laugh as she drew a card, looking at Riley. "So, what's it like being an officer here in Sandpiper Bay? You're probably bored out of your mind. Martha told me you're from Phoenix."

Riley had to draw two when it was her turn. Sandpiper Bay had been far from boring. "It's different than Phoenix. Smaller, more intimate. I enjoy being part of the department with Matthew, Rosita, and Nancy."

"What about Bradley?" Alf asked. His card skipped Matthew and it was Susan's turn.

"The chief is all right," Riley said, keeping her tone light. "I think I'm growing on him. He's in Bangor right now with his granddaughters. Triplets."

Gloria and Winston exchanged a look, then Winston said, "I volunteer at the fire station. Heard a rumor about a guy missing the other day. Any news?"

"A missing man?" Martha queried, turning to her son. "Matthew, do you know about that?"

"Mom, you know I can't discuss things at home." Matthew

played his next to last card. "Uno."

The goal of the game was to play until you had no more cards in your hand.

"I hate that rule. Your honorary uncle LaSpada used to bounce ideas off us when he was chief," Alf complained. "What night did this man go missing?"

Matthew and Riley said nothing.

Winston said, "Friday night."

"Winston!" Matthew said.

"The reason I'm bringing it up is because Gloria here saw a man without a jacket running across our yard. Makes me think about getting a fence."

"When?" Riley asked, lowering her cards.

"Friday night," Winston said, turning to his wife. "What time, hon?"

"I was up for a drink of water," Gloria said, excitement in her eyes, "at one, I think. I saw him clear as day. His back, anyway."

"Was he dressed?" Matthew blurted.

"What kind of question is that?" Martha reproved.

"What was he wearing?" Riley reworded.

"Jeans and a black shirt." Gloria put her cards down, the game forgotten. "Does that help?"

"But no jacket." Lars had been wearing jeans and a black Henley the night of the party. One in the morning would put him alive after leaving Coby's at midnight. Where had he been until then, and without his jacket?

"You didn't mention being on a case, Mom," Kyra said with a slight pout.

"We had enough going on with the weather. I don't like to bring my work home; you know that."

Kyra shrugged. "Did you find the guy yet?"

Riley hesitated before saying, "We are still conducting interviews. Thank you, Gloria and Winston, for your help."

"Who is it that's missing?" Martha asked.

"Lars Sorenson," Winston said. "Right, Matty?"

Matthew glanced at Riley and then around the table, his gaze landing on Winston. "We haven't broadcasted his disappearance because of the impending storm—as a volunteer firefighter, I'm sure you can appreciate the need to keep our citizens calm."

Winston agreed. "No sense in panicking, that's true. But now that the cat is out of the bag, what can you tell us? We can keep a secret."

Riley stifled a laugh.

Matthew groaned and put his last card down. "I win. I think it's time for bed."

The card players didn't budge. Kyra turned big eyes on Riley. "The creepy guy with the tattoos? That Lars?"

"Yes." Riley put a protective hand on Kyra's back.

"I didn't like him."

Martha chimed in with, "Lars was a rat, Kyra. You have good instincts. I met him when we were at Coby's for karaoke nights. He acted like he was God's gift to women." Martha gathered the cards and grinned to lighten the mood. "When everyone knows it's our Matty."

"Mom!" Matthew blushed a bright red and stood.

Heavy snow pounded the house and the wind howled overhead with cyclone force. Ice balls the size of a man's fist pelted the roof, the sides of the house, and the windowpanes. A gust blew down the chimney stack and the fire smoked inside the living room.

Riley tucked Kyra to her and assessed the situation, glad to be safe from danger. She took Susan's hand and the three of them said their goodnights, then rushed back to their room. Her mom and Kyra were sharing the double bed, and Riley the futon. Not that she expected much sleep. As a mother she'd be standing guard through the night.

"We are going to be fine," she told them. Kyra and Susan perched on the edge of the bed. The hail against the one window in the room had Riley fearing it might break. There was a room divider in the corner and Riley, with Kyra's help, wrestled it behind the dresser so that it was a barrier between the window and the room. "The windows are hurricane proof, so this is just a precaution."

The sound of the wind lessened. "That's better," Kyra said.

"Stay here. I'm going to help the others, but I'll be back. We have everything we need in this room. Headphones, snacks, water."

"Each other," Susan said, tugging Kyra back down to sit next to her.

"Hurry back, Mom."

She nodded and hustled down the hallway. Matthew and Alf, with Winston, were checking each window.

"Worth every penny of the remodel," Alf declared.

"I'm going to update our place with these too," Winston said. He reached for Gloria's hand, and she squeezed it.

"I agree! Oh, Matty, I'm so glad you're here too, and your friends. Riley, can we get you anything? We have a generator if we lose power so even if things go dark, it will just be temporary."

"Thank you for opening your home to us. I'm a light sleeper if anyone needs anything during the night." Riley raised her hand to the group and nodded at Matthew. Despite their best efforts, Lars's "disappearance" had surfaced—now they had another clue to add to the timeline of his death.

"See you in the morning, Harper." Matthew stayed in the living room, talking with his parents.

Riley joined her family and they talked about Uno and buying it for the house. Easy conversation that didn't block out the wind as it picked up speed and strength. Ice the size of soccer balls hammered the windows. The overhead light flickered.

"What are we going to do, Mom?" Kyra was trembling so bad that her teeth rattled. Susan patted her back.

"Let's turn out the light and get some rest," she suggested. All three of them kept their clothes on as they climbed beneath the covers. Riley turned off the switch.

Unfortunately, the dark seemed to amplify the shadows. Riley heard crackling noises above them and the weight of a tree falling nearby. Lighting strikes sounded so close she feared it had hit the house and got up from the futon to peer into the hallway.

"It's okay," Matthew assured her from where he'd come out of his room too. "I have a feeling that this mega storm will go down in history."

She said a little prayer that they would all survive it.

The force of nature showing its strength tonight was beyond anything she'd ever experienced. Riley had a vision of the angry sea slapping against the rocks—probably by now it had breached over the cliffs to flood the streets, turning the snow into ice and adding to the danger.

She returned to the room where her daughter was wide awake and sitting up. Susan held her close, and Riley sat on the other side of Kyra. This was her family. She would step in front of any disaster coming their way.

The three sat on the bed, holding hands. Hours passed. The wind was like an angry giant, battering the house. There was no break in the howling. Riley's nerves were taut but there was nothing they could do.

No yoga breathing was going to fix this situation.

The nor'easter was unmerciful and unrelenting as it punched and pummeled their sanctuary. There was no peace to be found.

Kyra at last fell asleep from sheer exhaustion, and Riley tucked her daughter under the comforter. Susan dozed and made room, putting her arm around Kyra.

Riley stood and stretched her back as she chided herself for bringing them here. Uprooting her family from all that they knew, this exciting adventure had turned to disaster—the biggest mistake she'd ever made, though she tried her damnedest to do things right.

CHAPTER TWELVE

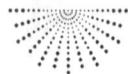

A SLIVER OF LIGHT CREPT AROUND THE ROOM DIVIDER SNUGGED against the window. Riley, who had stretched out on the futon, blinked her eyes and carefully sat up. Her mom and Kyra were both asleep. They'd made it through the night.

Thank the good Lord.

She tiptoed out of the room, wanting her family to get more rest. Riley was itching to see the damage. Following the smell of coffee, she wound up in the kitchen.

Matthew sat at the table, #1 Son mug in hand. "Morning," he said, rubbing his unshaved jaw. "We've got limited electricity due to the generator, but there's coffee and pastries."

"Heavenly. Thanks." She helped herself and sat next to him. She spoke quietly so as not to wake the others. "Have you had a chance to look outside?"

"I peeked out back. It's a freaking mess. Part of the neighbor's chicken coop is in our yard. There's a tree blocking the front door that just missed the chief's SUV." Matthew's ginger hair was standing on end; his sweet face hinted at sorrow. "And we were prepared. What about those that weren't?"

Riley understood. The island that he loved so much had

taken a beating. His job had been to protect it, but no one can combat a monster storm. "I'm sorry. Have you been in touch with anyone?"

He shrugged. "I used the radio to contact the chief, but it was a rotten connection. I'll try again when we get outside, maybe from the patrol car."

She nodded. "I don't hear the wind this morning. The quiet is eerie after such a crazy night."

"One of the worst I've been in," he said. He drained his mug and got up to refill it and hers.

"What's the plan, then? Check on the neighbors?"

Matthew blew out a breath and sank to his chair, a smile tugging his lips. "I like that nothing keeps you down, Harper."

She leaned forward and shared, "Don't get me wrong—I was shaking in my boots last night, certain I'd made a mistake in coming to Sandpiper Bay. But this morning, when the light came through the room divider, that negative energy disappeared. We'd made it through! I want to make sure that everyone else is also okay."

He raised his mug to her. "Once Dad and Winston wake up, we'll tackle tree removal and clear the front door. We have a chainsaw in the garage." The garage had an entrance from the house that he gestured to from his seat. "Snow is high as your knees. Power lines are down, and the live ones are extremely dangerous."

Riley stood up and began to pace, filled with the need to act. Once she determined that folks were safe, the knowledge that a killer was on the loose would take priority. "I don't know how to run a chainsaw, but maybe we could move the tree?"

"Hold on, hold on. Let me finish my coffee. This is going to be a heck of a long day."

She stepped toward the back door. "I'm going out to appraise the situation."

Matthew rocked back on his kitchen chair. "Not much you

can do. Why don't you work on the Lars investigation so that we can make headway? What did you think of Winston's bombshell last night?"

She zipped her boots and borrowed Matthew's coat. "Now we know that Lars was still alive an hour after he left Coby's, but he was missing his coat." Zeroing in.

"Yeah. What happened to it?"

"It was black leather. Not appropriate for winter, I remember thinking. It was more for style than function. Where does their yard open to? We can canvas the area around Winston and Gloria's place to see if he dropped it somewhere. Or the killer took it. We can't assume anything."

"Main street." He ruffled his hair. "This is Anchor, but they're on the other side."

Riley nodded. "A main thoroughfare. Coby lives a half-mile from the Lobster Pot. What if Lars panicked and ran someplace he thought might be open, but then he wakes up Shep, who barks and scares him off and he returns to Main. Tessa and Kimber both live within a few blocks. We need to mark a map of the neighborhood, Matthew."

"We have them at the station." Matthew stood and opened the curtains over the kitchen window. The snow was so bright it was blinding. It covered every surface. "We need to find this guy *and* focus on helping the islanders."

"Okay, I'll put my mastermind to work and see if I can solve this mystery while you're playing lumberjack. But first, I want to see what it's like outside."

"Suit yourself, but you won't get far with snow up to your knees." Matthew leaned against the counter.

"Is there any coffee left?" her mother asked from behind her. Without waiting for a reply, Susan went to the carafe and poured herself a cup.

"Hi, Mom. We survived." Riley shrugged out of Matthew's coat, skipping her outdoors idea. "Kyra still sleeping?"

"Out like a light. It was a rough night, so I don't blame her. What are you two talking about?"

"Lars's disappearance."

Her mom selected a croissant and sat down. "That was sure something last night about Winston and Gloria seeing him in their yard. Does that help you?"

Riley couldn't give or discuss details of the murder, but she could certainly continue with the disappearance charade. As Winston had said last night, the cat was out of the bag.

"It does, yes. But why don't we go into the living room and chat before the fire so that we don't wake anybody else?"

Matthew ushered them out of the kitchen. "I already added a few logs. I'll make another pot of coffee. Listen for the radio, all right? Chief could be trying to get in touch, among other folks."

She lifted the radio and put it in her left hand, holding her coffee mug in her right. "You got it."

A few minutes later, Gloria and Martha joined them, bringing a loaf of sliced banana bread to the coffee table. Winston, Matthew, and Alf could be heard outside before the front door. In between the whirring and buzzing of the chainsaw, the ladies discussed Lars.

"Where could he have gone?" Riley asked them. "I've checked with Tessa Barton, his prior landlady, and Kimber, the other bartender at The Shack." She also mentioned Emily Hamilton and the Hamilton family.

"Lindsay," Gloria said as she slapped her knee. "She's always been too perfect, you know? Until she wasn't."

"What do you mean by that?" Riley picked up a pen and positioned it over her paper tablet.

"Going to church every Sunday and bragging about it like she's better than us when we go to the same place! Well...Joan Higgins told me that she noticed Lindsay arguing with Lars after the service. Not that Lars went, mind you." Gloria practically puffed her chest with pride at being able to give another piece of the puzzle. Possibly. "They each were flinging their arms heatedly."

Joan was excellent at noticing things, so Riley wrote the tidbit down to be corroborated later. "Interesting. Do you know when this happened?" Had Lars been in town before this Friday?

Gloria preened. "Had to be around the end of September because we were collecting for the harvest party."

Kyra joined them, her hair escaping from its braid. "Morning. What are you talking about?"

"Lars," Martha said. "Would you like some breakfast, hon?"

Kyra glued herself to Riley's side, eyes and ears pinned to what was going on. "Not right now, thank you."

"I just can't agree with you, Gloria." Martha sipped from her mug. "I've known that family for a great many years and Lindsay had to have a reason for that outburst. She was probably warning Lars to stay away from Emily."

The other women nodded, including her mother. As a mom, Riley would move mountains if she detected a threat to her family.

It made sense. She decided that she would pay the Hamiltons a visit as soon as the chief's SUV was clear, no matter that she would be unwelcome.

The radio made an obnoxious beep that had Riley scrambling up from the couch to answer it. She brought the device to her mouth and clicked the button on the side. "Harper here." It crackled. She wandered to the back porch. Matthew had shoveled, creating a path to the lawn and around the house, probably to the garage and front driveway.

"Barnes. How's it going?"

She pressed in the button. "We're alive. We haven't been able to check on the neighbors yet..." The sound of chainsaws and generators filled the air.

"And the investigation?"

She shivered in the chill outside. The thermometer on the porch shaped like an anchor read thirty-eight degrees. "We found a cigarette butt and crushed cell phone that we believe might belong to Lars. Unfortunately, it was smashed." She sighed. "We have a witness that can place Lars outside around one Saturday morning. Sir, this would be a lot easier if we can confirm that Lars is dead. Rumors are rampant!"

"Fair enough. You can confirm his death on a need-to-know basis."

Her shoulders bowed with relief. "Have you heard from Dr. Lakshmi?"

"No," he barked. "What's your plan for the day? I know lines are down, and trees, but I expect you to be working the case—not sitting around like a lump on a log."

Riley heard the underlying frustration in his voice and didn't take offense. "Once the roads are cleared, I'm going to the Hamiltons. I need to talk with both Emily and Ryker. Lindsay too. After that, I'll check in with Bernie and Sally Murphy to see if any boats left the marina." She understood being busy, but she wouldn't leave until she got an answer.

"Good. Stay safe out there, Harper—but find me that killer." He mumbled a curse. "If I have to drop from an air glider I will be there as soon as there's a break in the weather."

He ended the conversation and Riley went back inside to warm up by the fire. The ladies all looked at her expectantly. "That was the chief, checking to make sure we're all right," she said, putting the radio on the charge station.

Just then the front door opened, and Matthew poked his head in, his cheeks flushed and eyes sparkling. "Free at last!"

She grinned at her partner. "Great timing. How long before the roads are drivable? Chief wants us to hit the ground running."

The guys came in behind Matthew and Alf clapped his son on the shoulder. "I heard Crash's plow out on Main Street a block over. We've got the snowblower and can have the driveway cleared in half an hour."

"That's great!" Riley said, realizing she wouldn't be quite as trapped as she'd feared.

Winston chimed in with, "I bought a wide shovel for my 4 by 4 a few years back. I can get you to the main road in twenty minutes. Most folks with trucks are happy to spend a grand or less on 'em, because ain't nobody likes to be stranded."

"Nope," Alf agreed. "I already checked, and there are no power lines down on our block—that's the real hassle right there. Never touch one," he told Riley, looking around Riley to make eye contact with Kyra and Susan too.

"We won't," Kyra said.

"If the vehicles get stuck," Gloria offered from her seat on the couch, "you're welcome to use our snowmobiles for the day."

That would be yet another first, patrolling by snowmobile. Riley thanked them all. "I'll go get my uniform on and meet you here, Matthew."

Riley dressed quickly, half expecting for Kyra to want to go home but both members of her family were happily chatting in the living room with the others.

"We're fine here, Riley," her mom said. "Martha's invited us for as long as we need."

"Thanks!" Riley saw that Kyra had her book at her side and a full cup of cocoa. "I appreciate all of your help. We'll be in touch when we can."

Kyra waved at her, and she and Matthew stepped out of the door. Crisp cool air stung her lips and her lungs. The skies were blue-gray and clear. Snow covered everything. Most of the trees had white on them. A few of the weaker ones had fallen over and would need to be removed. Neighbors had shovels and snowblowers and were pitching in to help each other. Winston had used the plow on his truck to make a single lane down their block to the main road. While Crash might be the only official snowplow on the island, many people had them.

"Is it over?" she asked. "The storm?"

"Don't know yet," Matthew said. "We can ask Wyatt later."

"Okay." She stuffed her hands in her jacket pockets and watched a neighbor shovel a path to the sidewalk. Another dragged broken branches to the side of their home. "Chief said we can share that Lars is dead on a need-to-know basis. I want to talk to the Hamiltons... What about you?"

Matthew checked his watch. "It's ten already. I'd like to drive to the library and make sure those folks are okay, then chat with Wyatt for a weather update before I go to the station."

"Great idea. Since I'll be by the marina to visit the Hamiltons, I'll talk to Bernie about the boats leaving the island. Does he have a record?"

"Not sure. Normally the marina would open at six for breakfast, but today, who knows? I've never known them to be closed." Matthew crossed his arms, thick in his winter jacket. "I'll check in on Coby too and see if Lars had an overnight bag or suitcase."

"Detective work is like collecting all of these parts and trying to see what fits." Riley palmed the keys to the SUV. "Let's reconvene at the station once we complete our interviews."

"Good luck!" Matthew got into his sedan and drove toward the station, following the lane that Winston had created.

Riley followed in his tracks until they reached the main road. Huge snowbanks were on either side. It was a relief to see that Crash had managed to clear two lanes on Main Street. Matthew turned one way and she went the other.

Time ticked and she was aware that she had to hurry. Killers didn't wait for anybody.

As she drove toward the marina, passing neighborhoods, she saw a few folks on snowshoes or cross-country skis, but for the most part the island was quiet.

Her skin dotted with goose bumps as she passed Mackabee Woods on Park Road. There was something about that forest that creeped her out. "Stop it, Riley."

It was eerie, no doubt. Was the killer hiding in the protection of thick trees? She imagined Ryker and his friend, Dorian, trying to follow Lars—tough teens, but not killers. Did they see themselves as protectors? Why had Ryker been in the woods? She didn't buy that he just wanted to sleep outside, alone. She was curious enough to do an internet search on the show.

The Hamilton house was in a neighborhood adjacent to the park, but she followed her instinct to chat up Sally and Bernie Murphy before conversing with the family.

Only two cars were at the waterside marina that had many long docks and several larger vessels anchored. A half-dozen men in knit hats and heavy jackets were smoking cigarettes outside the warehouse, arguing about who knew what.

Riley wanted to find out—and this time she actually had a card to play.

Bernie Murphy waved to her as he walked out of the market portion of the warehouse. Sally was probably inside the shop, ringing up orders.

"Officer Harper! How are you this morning? I was just going to call down to the station."

She drew up in surprise. "You were? Why is that?"

"One of my boats is missing. Probably lost in the storm but the owners are furious, not remembering they signed a contract that we have no responsibility. It costs them if they want us to move the boats into storage." He blew out a frosty breath. "In order for them to claim insurance, I've got to file a police report."

"Is that one?" Riley pointed to a yacht-sized boat that had no illusions of grandeur. Painted dark gray and white with wooden masts, it bobbed in the water of the bay.

"No, no. That's a shrimping boat." He gestured for her to

follow him around to the back of the warehouse and gestured to a bright-red dingy. "It was that size. We use them to fetch the lobster pots. Guy is making a fuss, and it's not worth more than two grand."

Riley walked over to the dock and gasped at the cold gusts of air that chilled her to the core. She clapped her gloved hands together and stomped her feet.

"I've got pictures of the boat inside," he said, understanding her reaction. "This must be some change from Phoenix."

"It is." She smiled. "It's just me and Officer Sniders at the station today—if you want to fill one out there."

"Oh, it's fine until tomorrow. I'm so annoyed at the guy that it might be fine till next week." He laughed, good humor restored. "Let's go inside and Sally can pour you a hot cup of joe."

That sounded heavenly. "Thanks so much."

"What brought you down here this morning? I know it wasn't about the stolen boat."

"No, but I did have a question concerning Lars Sorenson, and if any boats had been taken out in the early morning hours Saturday."

Bernie clamped his mouth tight but his expression exuded curiosity. Normally the man was as talkative as a parrot.

"What have you heard around the marina?"

Bernie said nothing. He was probably an excellent poker player for all his love of chattering. Only giving away what he wanted you to know—kind of like Nelson Bach.

"Just between you and me," Riley said in a low voice, "Lars is at the morgue. I was wondering if you could tell me what you knew about the man? His friends on the island here."

Bernie steered her close to the wall for privacy and didn't look the least surprised at the news. "Lars didn't have a lot of those," he conceded, slowing his pace as they neared the warehouse.

"Names?"

"Nelson and Crash were drinking buddies, but I don't think close friends. Lars preferred the ladies."

She'd already talked with Nelson and Crash. "They played cards together, right? With Charlie, Trevor, and Miguel too?"

"Ayuh." He smoothed blunt fingers over his jaw.

"And what ladies have you seen him talk to?"

He shrugged awkwardly. "Sally would be able to tell you that better than me."

Which implied that there were probably quite a few. "Thanks, Bernie. I'll ask her. Oh—about the boats in the marina? Do you have a record of what vessels left Friday and Saturday?"

"I can bring that to you when I file the claim for the stolen boat."

"Thanks. And please try to keep our conversation between us."

"Sure." At last, they reached the warehouse and passed the line of craggy-faced fishermen shooting the breeze despite the frigid temperatures.

"Morning, Officer," they chorused.

"Morning." She followed Bernie into the warmth of the shop and almost sighed with pleasure.

"Sally, love, Officer Harper has some questions for you."

"Sure!" Sally saw Riley's face, probably blue from cold, and poured steaming coffee into a to-go cup. "Here you are. Cream or sugar?" She pointed to the long counter with coffee and tea accoutrements.

"Thank you." Riley added cream and sipped. "You are a lifesaver."

Bernie chuckled and hustled outside back to work.

Sally came around the shop counter and straightened the napkins. Customers were on the far side looking at Murphy Marina dry goods.

"I'm surprised you're open," Riley said. "I expected everything to be shut down. Instead, every other neighbor has a snowplow, a snowblower, or a snowmobile." She laughed. "It's impressive."

"When you live in this kind of weather, you adapt to it. Last night's storm was a rough one though, and folks are coming here to make sure that everyone's okay." Sally greeted the next customer. "Morning, Lou."

The older man saw Sally talking to Riley, nodded, and went off to browse the soup section.

"He can wait a sec," Sally said. "What's up?"

Riley appreciated Sally's consideration. "As you probably already know, Lars Sorenson is missing."

Sally's brow arched. "I heard dead."

That was blunt and to the point. Riley nodded once. "The matter is currently under investigation. I was hoping you could tell me who his friends on the island were—especially the female ones."

"He had a long line of women willing to overlook his faults." Sally shook her head. "I don't care how good-looking you are, if you can't hold a job? No, thank you."

"I know of three women right now that I can connect to him."

Sally straightened the T-shirts on a shelf. "Locals then, not the tourists that he treated like a candy shop."

Riley sighed. "You're right. That would be a never-ending supply." She sipped and let the steam warm the tip of her nose.

"Tessa," Sally said in a quiet voice. There were stacks of gray and blue, next to white and red shirts.

Riley nodded and held up two fingers. "Kimber."

Just then the Hamilton ladies walked in, snowshoes over their shoulders. Lindsay and Emily were the same height, and both were pretty women. Emily had a fullness to her features while Lindsay's was more delicate.

Age had been kind.

"Emily," Riley murmured, keeping her gaze on the pair.

Sally snickered. "Not just Emily."

Riley was left openmouthed as Sally greeted her customers. Gloria had said that Lindsay had been yelling at Lars. What if she hadn't been protecting her daughter, but having a lover's spat?

CHAPTER THIRTEEN

Riley shut her mouth before she caught flies.

Where had that awful saying come from? Forget the saying. Sally had just implied that Lars had slept with both Emily and her mother.

If it were true and Sam, husband *and* father, had discovered this, it would be one hell of a motive for murder.

"Hi there!" Lindsay said to Riley. She was slender even in her thick jacket, her dark-blond hair combed back into a ponytail. She was probably forty, like Riley.

Riley cleared her mind and sipped her coffee so she could manage, "Hello!" without sounding strained.

Emily flipped her long shiny ponytail and half smiled, half smirked at Riley. "Officer."

"Something wrong, Sally?" Lindsay asked, going to the cooler for a jug of milk. "What an awful storm."

"Oh no…" Sally glanced at Riley, in full uniform, then said, "We have a dingy missing. Probably should have been put away before but…"

She owed Sally one for covering why Riley might be there at the marina.

"That storm last night was *wicked*. Thought we were all going to die. Everything in the house shook. Our windows were getting blasted. Did you hear that fricking hail? It was like footballs smashing into us," Emily stated with excitement. "I wouldn't expect to see that boat again. Except in pieces."

"Emily thought we were going to lose all the shingles from our roof, the wind was so strong," Lindsay said. "It howled and the puppy howled along with it."

Lindsay brought the jug to the counter and put it down, then walked to the shelves of pasta and Velveeta.

"We need comfort food after such an awful night," Emily explained to Sally. "Get two, Mom."

Laughing, Lindsay toted the items to the counter. "Anything else? Oh, Ryker wanted Doritos."

"We only have the Ranch flavor; is that all right?" Sally asked, heading toward the shelves.

"It will have to be." Lindsay paid for the items. "It's so beautiful outside. You can hear the birds chirping from the woods."

"Except for Dad out back with the chainsaw. *Vrooom, vroom!*" Emily took one of the bags.

"Did you have a lot of damage?" Sally asked, concern in her tone.

"No," Lindsay said. "Two trees knocked over in the back of the property—no biggie. A couple of shingles. Our house made it through just fine. Poor Randy and Carol next door lost part of their roof! Sam helped them first thing this morning with a tarp."

"Ryker too," Emily said, giving her brother credit. "Until the puppy got hold of the rope, and Dad sent them both home again." She snickered.

Riley imagined that teen and dog were enthusiastic hindrances.

Emily stepped toward the door, the snowshoes over her shoulder bonking into Riley. "Oops! Sorry!"

"Your snowshoes are very clever," Riley said. This close, Emily's skin and hair shone with good health.

"We sell them, if you want to try 'em out." Sally handed Lindsay the last bag of items and rounded the counter.

"It's easy when you get the hang of it," Lindsay said. "It's nice to be mobile—you don't feel quite as landlocked."

Sold! "Sally, I'll take three pairs."

Mother and daughter had the same sunny grins as they left with their goodies. Riley was glad she'd stopped at the marina before going to the Hamiltons. Now she needed to touch base with Matthew and go over what she'd learned. It might be best for them both to go to the house a little bit later.

"Sally, I don't mean to be rude...but have you noticed anything different about Emily in the last few months?"

"Like what?"

Riley had a hunch about something. "Her complexion, her clothes..."

"She's put on a few pounds, but it'll fall off once she's more active. I gained twenty pounds after high school." Sally sighed. "All I did was watch television and eat junk."

"It's so easy to do!" Riley paid for the snowshoes and looked around to make sure they were alone. "Do you think that anybody else might have noticed Lars with Lindsay? Joan Higgins mentioned them together too. Did I understand you correctly?"

Sally put the snowshoes in a bag that read Murphy's Marina. "I think it was six months ago that I saw Lindsay and Lars out on the dock—they did that thing where they touched fingers as if they wanted to hold hands but knew someone might see them. Stupid. What if I had been Sam, or their kids? Ryker is already high-strung."

"You know the family well."

Sally blinked. "Of course, I do. And now that you brought it up, there has been a change in Emily. She's calmed down since

Lars left. She used to hang out with him—not sure if he was seeing her mother at the time, or if that had already ended. He'd buy a couple beers and they'd sneak off into the woods. Lars was a bad influence," she said. "On everyone." She did a cross on her chest. "God rest his soul."

Riley nodded. "You've been an amazing help, Sally, thank you."

"You come back now, if you need a lesson with those snowshoes."

"Got it!" Riley left the shop and headed for the SUV. No cell service, again. Once inside, Riley radioed Matthew.

Where was the killer? It seemed Lars'd had no friends and yet four women on this island had a relationship with him. Was somebody sheltering him?

Riley felt cold to the bone.

Matthew picked up. "Sniders here."

"Hey! How's it going? I've got all kinds of news."

"Oh?" Matthew cut her off. "Me too. I'm sitting with Coby right now. Any chance you can stop by the medical center to talk with Dr. Lakshmi? Chief said she had something she wanted to show us. Then come here, okay?"

Interesting. Yep. The Hamiltons could wait. "You got it."

Riley reached the main road toward the medical center which was plowed but still required her to drive carefully. She didn't even want to think about her Fiat in these conditions. She parked next to the ambulance that had picked up Lars. Since then, there had been so many questions and very few answers.

She went inside. Serge and Trevor were hanging out in the lobby watching a movie on the television, as relaxed as if they were in their own homes. Why weren't they?

"Hello, guys. Everything all right?"

This Monday was a holiday and normally the medical center would be closed unless there was an emergency. Maybe there had been casualties due to the storm that had required Dr. Lakshmi to come in.

"Just killing time," Trevor said. He stretched his legs out and waved at Riley. "Hey."

Serge shifted on the industrial sofa. "Got the radio on if we're needed. Me? I'm glad for a little downtime between emergencies. Had two so far today but nothing major."

"They're mostly keeping me company," a female voice said from behind her.

Riley turned. A petite woman with dark hair and eyes, olive skin, and very white teeth smiled sheepishly. "You must be Dr. Lakshmi."

"I am. I hate to be alone in this big old place. It's usually full of voices but..."

Riley recalled what Serge had told her and said, "You drew the short stick?"

"I did." Her smile widened. "Call me Pru."

"I'm Riley Harper."

"The new officer on the island. I've heard about you, and it's nice to meet you officially. Matthew is probably getting very impatient with me. I've been the only one on duty. This morning has been blessedly light. A broken arm to set, stitches. Due to the storm, I expected more injuries. Not to complain! This way."

Pru whirled and her physician's coat floated out behind her like a white cape.

"What did you find with Lars?" Riley needed to know what he'd been holding. It might be a clue to identify his killer.

"Come with me, Officer, and I will show you." Pru hurried down the linoleum hall lit by fluorescent tubes. Rubber soles squished against the floor.

"Thanks." Riley's work boots didn't make the same noise. "We appreciate anything you can tell us about how Lars died."

"These are all preliminary findings until I finalize my

report." Pru pushed open a gray metal door. "It's a terrible thing, what happened to him."

"It's the worst I've ever seen." Riley would never forget Lars and how he'd been found in the snowbank, frozen. Naked.

Pru went into another room that was very cold, using her shoulder to swing it wide. "I imagine you see quite a bit of violence in your line of work."

Riley continued after the doctor. "I do. This part never gets easier." This was about finding a murderer.

Pru pulled back a blue sheet that had covered Lars Sorenson, baring his chest. Riley kept her gaze on his dark hair. Fixed eyes in a pale face. The marks around his neck from where he'd been choked had darkened. His skin was marble-white.

Her stomach roiled but settled down. This was part of the job. She breathed in and out, in and out. *Calm. Observe. Study. Look for answers.*

The doctor slipped on rubber gloves and pointed to the discoloration on his cheekbones. "He was hit. Punched repeatedly."

Riley stepped closer. If she didn't think of Lars as a breathing person, she could compartmentalize. "Was he in a fight, or was he beaten to death?"

Pru raised Lars's hands, tracing the knuckles. "See this?"

"The tattoos?" *L O V E* and the card symbols. The right hand was not closed as tightly as it had been.

"No. The bruising along the tattoos. He punched as well as *got* punched." The doctor shifted the sheet. "I don't know if it's related to his death."

"That makes sense with what I've heard about him." Coby and Miguel had both been in physical altercations with him. "He drank and got into brawls."

Pru then lowered the sheet to his calves, showing punctures on the hip and leg that Riley hadn't seen before. "Serge told me that he was found by the side of the road, dug up by the plow?

The thing is, there are no marks for him to have been dragged by a blade. These are animal bites of some kind. I believe he was mauled *after* he was already dead, which means that he could have been killed in a different spot than where he was found."

The island had cougars, wolves, and coyotes. Riley eyed the hand again. "Doctor, he was holding something. Did you discover what it was?"

"Yes." The doctor retrieved a plastic bag from the counter with a single black hair and handed it to Riley.

"Is that human?" Riley asked, studying the straight strand. She ran through the folks in town with black hair. There were plenty to choose from—Katie for one, but hers was curly. Don's too. More important, Miguel Garcia had black hair, and he'd been in a brawl with Lars. Ripples of adrenaline raced across her skin.

"No. It's an animal hair but I don't know what kind yet. I'm going to send it to the mainland for tests." Pru held out her hand and Riley gave the strand back.

Not human. And the excitement at tracking a murderer through DNA evidence came to a halt. "Could it be from the animal that mauled him?"

"It's possible. There *is* something else that I found, in his mouth." Riley looked at Lars and then the doc. Pru chose another plastic bag and showed it to Riley.

It was a card, wadded up. The king of spades. "This was *in* his mouth?"

"Shoved with a lot of force," the doctor said. "I don't know the lore, but I've heard that the king of spades represents death."

Riley swallowed and handed the envelope back to the doctor. Andy Garcia had had a deck of cards on his register at the liquor store, next to his smokes.

"How did he die? Was he choked to death with the card, and then by someone's hands?"

The doc lifted her shoulder, not committing. "It looks that

way, but I want to wait for the results of the blood tests to come back first."

Riley tried to imagine Lars's last hours. "Is it possible that he could have died from exposure to the weather?"

"That is not what happened here. Lars was killed, and then left outside. My estimate is that he'd been in extreme temperatures for less than seven hours." Pru peered up from Lars's body.

Seven hours. Riley and Matthew had discovered the body at nine in the morning. That would put his death around two.

"Thank you, Doctor. You've been very helpful. Will you let me know as soon as you get the tox screen back, as well as the fur strand?"

"Yes, of course. Chief Barnes is having a conniption over this taking so long but what can we do?" The little doctor shrugged, then tugged off her gloves and tossed them in the trash. She washed up and dried her hands.

Riley really liked this woman. "The chief will be back tomorrow."

"Excellent." Pru turned and changed into a different white coat. "The report should be done by next week. No internet means no lab results from our sister hospital in Bangor."

"I'll explain that you are doing all you can."

The pair walked down the aisle to the lobby. The paramedics had gotten up for coffee and chips from the vending machine.

"Doc, you want the cheddar squares or the spicy trail mix?" Serge offered them both to Pru.

"Spicy trail mix. Thanks, Serge." Pru grinned at Riley's expression. "I'm a junk food junkie. This stuff keeps me going."

Everyone had a vice or two, it seemed. "I hope you don't have to be here much longer?"

"Another hour for paperwork. It's amazing how much I can accomplish without a lot of folks around, but I wanted to come in and get back to you about Lars."

"Thank you." Riley turned to Serge and Trevor, who slurped

from paper coffee cups. "You guys have a nice day. Trevor, you were right about the storm hitting. Any word on when the weather is supposed to clear?"

"I was talking to Crash, and he and Wyatt think by Tuesday," Trevor said. "The storm's gone and now we have to clean up the mess."

She supposed that both being captains, one a tugboat, the other for a ferry barge, they had the same restrictions on water safety. It wasn't surprising that everybody knew one another. "Can I get Crash Moreno's cell phone number?"

Both Trevor and Serge nodded, but Trevor beat Serge to pulling up the contact on his phone. "No cell service, so you'll have to jot this down the old-fashioned way."

Serge chuckled. "Where would we be without technology?"

Riley didn't want to know. She liked regular internet and cell towers that worked. This storm had shown her that she couldn't rely on cyberspace.

They wandered to the empty receptionist's desk where Trevor set his paper coffee cup down, scored a pencil, and wrote the number and address down for Riley on a Post-it.

"If he's not driving the snowplow, he'll be home," Trevor said. "Remember, by the woods?"

She recalled the day that Ryker had gone missing with crystal clarity when Crash and Shazam had showed up to help find the missing teen. The Hamiltons flashed like neon on her suspect list.

"And Crash knew Lars," Riley said. She needed to find out why Lars would return to a place where he was hated enough to be killed. "Did he owe Lars money, or did Lars owe him money? From cards?" Why the king of spades?

Pru grew more attentive to the conversation.

Serge wiped a hand down his face. "Crash was really upset about Lars being caught in his plow. Finding someone that way… It's a shock, you know?"

"And how did he find that out?" Riley asked, showing her disapproval. "I wanted you to keep that under your hat."

"Trevor," Serge said, throwing his pal under the bus. "He couldn't believe that Crash didn't know a dead body was in that pile of snow."

Trevor flushed a dark red color. "Sorry. I forgot."

"The two of them were drinking, that's what happened." Serge chuckled. "Whiskey makes for loose lips."

Pru cleared her throat. "It's too bad that happened, Trevor, but do you know anything that Officer Harper might use for the investigation?"

Trevor grabbed his coffee, thinking hard. "Well, he said it was snowing so thick that he didn't notice anything wrong—he was telling the truth. Me, Crash, Nelson, and Miguel all play poker together. I'd vouch for them all. They're my friends."

Riley exhaled and pocketed the information about Crash. "I wish things worked that way. Thanks, all of you. Doctor, let's stay in touch."

She left the building wanting to throttle Trevor—even as she was glad he'd given her Crash's address and phone number. It wasn't until she'd almost reached the police station that she realized that they hadn't answered her question about the money.

CHAPTER FOURTEEN

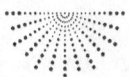

RILEY PARKED AT THE FRONT ENTRANCE TO THE POLICE STATION
and noticed a set of snow skis propped up outside. The
islanders were nothing if not adept at dealing with the weather.

The skis against the wall had to belong to Coby, she thought.
She planned on asking the bar owner exactly who else Lars
might have had a fight with. From what she'd seen of Coby's
knuckles, and Lars's, neither had been bruised at dinner.

She walked in with purpose and a question in her mind.

"Hi, Riley," Coby said, his expression serious and very unlike
his normal jubilant self. "I'm glad you're here."

"Why's that?" She stiffened her spine while keeping a neutral
outward demeanor. *Please don't confess to killing Lars.*

Matthew straightened in his chair and studied Coby.

Coby sank down, his hands in his hair. "I feel terrible about
this." He sucked in air and then said, "Kimber lied to you. About
Lars."

Relief almost buckled her knees, but she kept up the tough
act. "Oh?"

"Yeah." Coby tapped his fingers to his knee with nervous
energy. "I told her to drop in and come clean, but she's afraid."

163

"Why would Kimber be scared of talking to the police? I was already at her house, and we had a nice conversation. Very cordial." Riley crossed her arms. The thickness of her coat made it awkward, so she lowered them and unzipped the front.

"One night after work—this was a week before Lars took off for Bangor, and I think was part of the reason he left—the two of them got into a screaming match at the bar. I guess she caught him stealing money from her purse."

Kimber had mentioned that. So far, Coby's story tracked with what the bartender had already told her.

"And?"

Coby rubbed his Adam's apple in a nervous gesture. "The screaming turned physical. The bar was already closed so there weren't any customers. I heard yells and cussing from the back room, so I came out as Kimber vaulted over the bar top with a bottle of Seagram's and clonked him. Hard."

Riley glanced at Matthew. His slack jaw conveyed his surprise about Kimber hitting Lars over the head with a bottle. "What happened?"

"Lars went down, and Kimber was immediately contrite, you could see, but Lars got up, shook himself off, and threw his weight against Kimber." Coby straightened, in protector mode. "He was furious. I got between them and put him in a chokehold."

Had this led to the fistfight between Lars and Coby that the chief had mentioned?

"And it escalated?" Riley asked. How bad had the fight been?

Coby rubbed his knuckles. "Yeah. I wasn't going to let Lars beat up Kimber. Not happening in my bar!" His bravado faded quickly, and he ran his palm over his face. "Not one of my finer moments."

The night Coby had been robbed, had it happened how Coby said, that he'd heard Lars and gone to see what he was up to? Was he defending himself? Dr. Pru had showed her that Lars had bruises on his skin from a fight.

Matthew jotted down a note on his tablet. "Kimber and Lars had a relationship?"

"No, Matthew, it was just sex. They'd been hooking up occasionally with no expectations. Kimber's a good girl, but young and not overly selective." Coby shrugged, not judging.

The way he said that immediately bought Emily to Riley's mind.

Emily might have been a good, sweet girl, also caught in Lars's snare. Riley wanted to hustle Coby out the door so she could discuss the recent facts with Matthew.

Stay in the moment, Riley. You can't let him loose yet. "Coby, did you and Lars get into a fistfight the night he stole from you?"

Coby flushed. "No. I told you this already."

"Did Lars have a suitcase when he stayed with you, or a bag with his clothes, and personal items?"

"Nothing." He frowned. "That's weird, huh?"

She believed Coby. Nothing in his nature suggested payback or murderous tendencies. The slim proof she was holding on to was that Coby had no bruises on his knuckles.

"I wish you'd gone to Maria's." For an alibi.

"I was going to—but no way could I let Lars stay in my house without me. And look what happened anyway!"

Riley watched Coby carefully. "Does the king of spades mean anything to you?"

He scowled with confusion. "No."

"This may come as a surprise to you." Or not. "Lars is dead, Coby."

Coby's jaw tightened but he didn't avert his gaze. "I'd heard a rumor."

It was half past twelve, and Riley didn't want to waste more time on Coby when her focus needed to be finding the murderer.

"Did you talk to Emily already?" Matthew asked Riley, blurring the line of his friend Coby and his job for a moment.

"Not yet." Riley glanced from Matthew to Coby. "Coby, thank you for bringing this to our attention. Do you think that Kimber had a reason to take out her anger on Lars that night?"

"No. I really don't. Kimber and Tamara had each other's backs and made it clear they wanted nothing to do with him. I told him he wasn't welcome at the bar, not even as a customer. Kimber knew my decision."

Riley nodded. Coby didn't have bruises on his knuckles. She was going with her intuition. He hadn't killed Lars.

Had Kimber? Would she be physically capable? Or had she been helped by her best friend? They were tight and told each other everything. Riley thought back to the party and then the interview at her house. Neither woman had injuries to their hands. However, until Riley had the killer in custody, everyone had to be a suspect.

"Can I have a word with you, in my office?"

"Yeah." Matthew pushed the paperwork about the theft across to Coby. "Why don't you read this to make sure it's correct? I'll be back in a second."

Riley led the way to her office, turned on the light, and shut the door after pulling Matthew in. She had so much to say, and too little time. "Obviously Lars was in a fight that he didn't win. Coby doesn't have bruises on his knuckles. Dr. Lakshmi says it's possible that Lars's body was moved by an animal. Cause of death is possible choking, but there was a king of spades playing card shoved in his mouth. It means death in some circles. We don't know where he was killed. It could have been anywhere on this island."

Matthew reeled backward in surprise. "That's a lot of info to add to the board. So, I can let Coby go?"

"Yes," Riley said. "Lindsay was having an affair with Lars." She didn't mention that she wondered if Emily could possibly be pregnant in case the young woman had only gained a few pounds. "What if Sam and Ryker decided to take care of family business? I was hoping you could come with me since we have multiple suspects in the same house."

"I have to stay here with Coby. Can you wait a while? I just need him to finish the report. Damn paperwork."

She was tempted, but time was passing in a flash. "Tell you what—I'll stop at Kimber's first to verify her story, and then you join me at the Hamiltons as soon as you're done with Coby. We should be there at the same time. We need to catch the killer, or killers, and they have answers."

Matthew opened her office door. "It's a plan. Be careful."

"See you! Bye, Coby." Riley hustled out the front door and returned to Kimber's, which was on the way to the Hamiltons. Nobody answered her knock.

She looked around the property and saw ski tracks, two sets, across the snow. True islanders didn't let bad weather keep them in for long.

Riley then drove to the Hamiltons. What would she say? What *could* she say? Now that she could let the murder be known, she could take a harder stance with the family.

She parked on the street with a view of the house to wait for Matthew. Ryker and Bear were outside, the black mutt pulling Ryker on a sled across the mounds of snow. The teen was laughing, and Riley's heart lifted.

This was the beauty in life—such a stark contrast to Lars, dead on a slab in the morgue. She focused on the laughter.

Using the radio, she dialed Matthew. He answered with a gruff, "Sniders."

"Where are you? I'm at the house."

"Changing a flat. I ran over a jagged strip of fallen roof metal —all part of cleaning up the island after a storm, but this is the worst timing. I tried calling Rosita, but she's probably avoiding us to have a day off."

"Matthew, don't worry. I'll go ahead and do the interview with the family, then check back with you. I'll be done by the time you're finished so don't come."

Riley studied the house. Fresh wood was stacked to the side. A blue tarp covered a portion of the neighbor's roof.

Slowly driving down the side road, she reached the Hamiltons' home, parked, and got out. It was time to take the bull by the horns.

She knocked on the front door and Sam answered with a surprised look on his handsome face. He was dressed in a plaid flannel shirt untucked over blue jeans. His feet were in thick socks.

"Hi. And a happy Monday morning to you." Sam widened the door. "Come on in."

She nodded, smiled, and stomped snow from her boots before entering the foyer.

It smelled like nutmeg and apple pie. Another of Emily's cravings?

Emily walked from the kitchen, carrying a bowl of cheesy pasta. "Confess, Officer Harper—you're here because you want my lunch."

"What? Don't be rude, Em," Sam said.

"Just a joke, Dad. Chill out." Emily dug her spoon into the bowl. "We saw the hardworking officer this morning at the marina when Mom and I were picking up snacks."

Father and daughter turned their eyes on Riley. She raised her chin. "Not here for lunch, I'm afraid. I have a few questions for you, Emily, that I'd like to ask in private. Take a walk with me?" Riley gestured to the front door.

"No way. It's freezing outside. I finally got warm from this morning." Emily brushed by Riley and her dad, her body cocooned in layers of sweaters over roomy yoga pants. "Come on up to my domain. We can be private there."

"Hey!" Sam said. "You can't—what is this about? I want to be part of this conversation. This is my house—and my daughter." He faced Riley. "Unless you have a warrant for her arrest, you have no right to barge in here, asking questions. This is the second time that you've abused our hospitality."

"Just relax, Dad. You're losing your mind these days."

Sam's face reddened at his daughter's disrespectful tone. "Young lady…"

"I'm an adult. Don't force me to move out right now because I will." Emily shoved a spoonful of pasta into her mouth and put a foot on the bottom stair of the staircase, her brow arched as she swallowed. "I can live with Bobbie Joe in Portland—she already said I could."

"Is that a threat?" Sam crossed his arms, obviously at a loss. His wayward daughter held all the power.

Would Sam be supportive of her if he discovered that Emily was pregnant?

Sam was big, bulky, muscular, and had a militant bearing. He was familiar with knives, fishing gear, and had the strength to follow through, unlike Kimber.

If he'd found out that his wife and his daughter had slept with Lars, that would be cause to want Lars dead.

Religious symbols hung on the walls. Prayers for wisdom and serenity. The family was known for their churchgoing ways.

Would Sam be able to forgive his wife's infidelity? Kill the man, not his wife.

Riley didn't flinch under Sam's withering glare. She needed to find out who had killed Lars Sorenson, and Emily hopefully had answers. Taking Emily to the station wouldn't serve in this situation, so they would all need to adapt.

Riley held her ground.

Sam cursed, turned on his heel, and slammed out the front door in his socks.

"Sorry about him," Emily said, cradling her bowl to her rounded chest. "I've been something of a disappointment."

Emily ambled up the stairs slowly until they reached the landing.

Riley took note of the spacious second floor that had a loft with a television and video games, a foosball table, and a tall cage with hamsters.

A room at the far end of the hall had a poster with a wizard dueling an alien—some video game probably, Riley thought. She recalled the sound of the window breaking on that side of the house a few days ago when Ryker had been missing.

This was Ryker's room.

Emily stepped toward the door with an artsy letter E on it in aqua blue. She opened it and ushered Riley inside.

"Come on in," Emily said, shutting and locking the door behind her. "This is the only way to get privacy around here. Hang on."

Emily put a record on a modern record player that Kyra wanted. It was a popular thing to have, just like an old type-writer. Kelly Clarkson sang about heartbreak.

A full-sized bed with an aqua net and white and blue comforter and pillows took up a corner by the window. It was covered with an aqua curtain.

"Take the chair. I'm into the bean bag these days." So saying, Emily plopped backward, placed her bowl down, and sighed as her body was enveloped in plush comfort.

Riley sat on the office chair before the desk, turning it around first so that she could look at Emily. She quickly perused the room for pictures. Lots with her girlfriends. None that were out in the open with Lars.

Did Emily know about her mom's affair, or had Lindsay managed to keep her secret?

Riley would tread carefully in order to not splinter the family further.

Emily scraped the last bit of pasta into her mouth and closed her eyes, enjoying the simple pleasure of her favorite food.

"Emily, I have a few questions…"

Emily's eyes flickered open with intelligence. "Yes?"

"You and Lars." How to tactfully bring up the pregnancy?

Emily's cheeks blushed pink. She was the epitome of good health and youth. "You know that we were in love?"

Kimber had told Riley that Emily believed Lars loved her. That she loved him. "You were?"

"Yep. Then he found out that I was knocked up." Her nose turned red.

Riley had been right. "Did Lars promise marriage?"

"No. He gave me two hundred bucks that he stole from Kimber and told me to *take care* of it."

Riley was appalled at this man's awful behavior.

Emily caught her up short when she said, "As if two hundred would be enough."

Riley reacted with a mother's heart when she needed to be a police officer.

Stay calm, stay calm, stay calm.

CHAPTER FIFTEEN

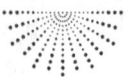

"You should see your face right now, Officer Harper."
Emily chuckled. "It's like you're sucking the entire box of Sour
Patch Kids."

Riley schooled her features, trying not to interpose Kyra on
that bean bag. Kyra also liked that particular candy. "I'm sorry.
So. You wanted to get an abortion?"

"What? Slow down, lady. I never said that. I'm totally gonna
keep it. I just haven't decided how to tell my folks yet." Her
mouth twisted. "I'm surprised they haven't noticed but they've
been arguing a lot, so their prodigal daughter probably isn't first
in their mind."

"Do your parents know about you and Lars?" Riley studied
the teen for any signs of heartbreak over him being dead but
didn't sense any.

Emily shrugged and crossed her arms behind her head, her
legs stretched out. "They think I had a crush. Ryker knows,
though, that it was more serious. He would cover for me when
I'd sneak out. When he's not being a dweeb he's pretty cool."

"Where did you meet?" Riley wanted confirmation of what
she'd deduced and wasn't surprised.

"Mackabee Woods."

Ryker could not be a killer. But Riley didn't hold fast to that —she was aware of plenty of murderers who weren't old enough to vote.

"The woods don't bother you?"

"They're creepy at night for sure, but that just made it more, you know, thrilling, I guess. Kinda dumb now. I know lots of people who don't like Lars, but I love him. I hope that he'll find out that I'm still pregnant—five months —and change his mind. I want him to marry me and take me away from here." Tears spurted from her eyes, and she wiped them free, sitting up awkwardly because of the bean bag.

"Emily, hon," Riley said. The tragedy of Lars's murder was compounded by Emily's loss of innocence in many ways, not just impending motherhood with no father.

It was possible that Ryker had killed Lars in defense of his sister—it was a motive that made unfortunate sense.

"What?" Emily sniffed.

"I have more questions about Lars, if you can answer them? Who were his friends, besides you?"

She shook her head. "We didn't hang out a lot—it was hard for me to sneak away, you know. We had our special spot in the woods that he'd make so romantic. Candles and a blanket. Beer." A sad smile flitted across her mouth. "I was a virgin, but he told me that he loved me and wanted to show it. He said so over and over again—even after. Usually when we were doing it, ya know?"

Riley stifled her anger at Lars for trifling with someone so innocent. If this was what she felt, she imagined that Ryker would feel the same. Sam Hamilton? Her belly clenched. Her compassion for Lindsay wasn't as strong.

"Did you know he was in town this past weekend?"

Emily stared down at her fingernails. "I thought I heard a

rock against my window, but in the storm I wasn't sure. When I looked outside, I didn't see him."

Had Lars come here after Coby had chased him out? "What time was that?"

Setting the empty bowl aside, Emily shrugged.

Ryker was a lean teen with muscle. He was familiar with an air rifle, and probably a knife. He fished with his father. Possibly hunted.

Her thoughts circled to Sam—a grown man. "Do you know why your parents have been fighting?"

Emily nibbled her fingernail. "Nope. I've been making backup plans with my friend Bobbie Joe, you know, just in case they kick me out."

"Do you want me to be with you when you tell them? There are plenty of places to go for healthcare and assistance."

A hard knock rapped against the wooden door. "Emily? What's going on?" The doorknob twisted and Lindsay said, "Let me in."

Riley stayed put—this was Emily's show.

Emily got to her feet with a nimbleness she would lose over the next few months. "Coming...chill out, Mom." She unlocked the door.

Lindsay burst into the room, almost knocking into Emily. "Dad said that the police are here?"

Emily glanced at Riley. "Mom, we need to have a family meeting. Officer Harper is going to stick around."

"She's not family." Lindsay smoothed her hair back in a nervous gesture.

"Mom! You get Ryker and Dad. We'll be right down. Kitchen table—I'm ready for that apple pie." Emily put her hand on her belly, but her mother was oblivious to the small clue.

"Officer Harper, what is this about?"

She came up with a fast plan to get the family all together. If

Sam or Ryker refused, that would show guilt. If they didn't, she could see their faces as they gathered around the table.

"Let's wait until we get downstairs. I think Emily is right, and everyone should be together."

Lindsay slid her arm around her daughter's shoulders. "Are you okay, honey? Are you in some kind of trouble?"

Emily led the way down the hall and then the staircase. Ryker and Sam were already in the kitchen where Ryker was tugging something from the dog's mouth. "Whatcha got, boy?"

Brown leather. What was that? A wallet?

"May I see that?" Riley said.

Ryker, raised to be polite, tugged it free at last and handed it over but Sam tried to stop him.

Riley snagged it and opened it. Lars Sorenson's cocky mug smiled back at her from his Maine driver's license. "*Where* did you find this?"

Ryker's eyes widened. Sam glared at Ryker. Lindsay paled as if she recognized the wallet.

"Answer, son." Sam slammed his open palm to the tabletop. The salt and pepper shook.

"I, I..." Ryker glanced toward Emily.

Emily raised her chin. "That's Lars's, my soon-to-be husband."

Riley put her free hand on Emily's shoulder. This was a difficult situation and about to get tougher. "Have a seat, Emily."

"What are you talking about, Emily?" Sam demanded. He'd changed his socks for slippers with thick rubber soles.

Lindsay winced and covered her hand with her mouth. She stepped back against the kitchen wall.

"We talked about this, Emily. Lars was too old for you. It was a crush. Besides..." Sam looked at Riley with a harsh glare. A man used to being in command. "It doesn't matter anymore."

Riley held Emily's hand, her gaze on the other members of

the Hamilton family. She needed clues. Tells. Who would show guilt? "Lars Sorenson is dead."

Lindsay didn't so much as flinch. Neither did Sam or Ryker. Emily, however, wailed her surprise and grief. "No! No…" She released Riley's hand and buried her head in her arms at the kitchen table.

Ryker snorted at his parents when they didn't offer comfort to his sister, then dropped to his knees beside her. Bear snuffled between the siblings, sensing sadness. "It's okay, Em." He patted her arm. She raised her bloodshot eyes.

"It's not, Ryker." Emily raised watering eyes. "I'm going to have a baby."

Riley squeezed Emily's shoulder in support, then stepped back. Sam wore an expression of grief and shock, while Lindsay seemed paralyzed at the news.

"Lars is the father?" Lindsay asked in a daze.

"We were going to get married. He loved me," Emily stated defiantly in that brash manner only someone so young could manage.

Riley cleared her throat to gain their attention and get the pressure off Emily. It was best to get these things out in the open and come together as a family—if that was possible. If one of them hadn't killed Lars. "You all knew he was dead," she stated. "Except for Emily."

Ryker straightened and nodded, rocking back on his heels. "Not at first. Crash and Nelson were at the marina with Bernie, talking about Lars missing."

"When was that?" Riley asked.

"Saturday morning. It's why I searched for him that night in the woods and got lost, as you know. Anyway, I never found him."

Her stomach clenched. Saturday morning, Lars was already dead. "When was the last time you saw him, Ryker?" Riley asked in a quiet voice. "Did you see him Friday night?"

Ryker stood and scuffed his boot to the hardwood floor. Bear stuck to his leg. "Yup. He was tossing stones at Em's window. It was real late, and he woke me up. I chased him off the property with my air rifle."

Emily gasped. "You scared him away? I thought you were on my side?"

"Sis, I love you, but Lars is bad news." Ryker, looking older than fifteen, asked Riley, "Did he freeze to death? I've been feeling so guilty. I heard this morning that he'd died but not how. I came home and told Dad."

Sam flicked his sorrowful gaze to Lindsay, who was pale and shaking. "Kids, you aren't the guilty ones. Damn, Lindsay, are you too selfish to help your own children right now?"

Riley stayed still. Sam knew about the affair. He believed in God and country—would he have taken the law into his own hands?

"It doesn't matter," Lindsay sobbed. "It's over."

Emily shifted on her chair. "Mom, what is Dad talking about?"

Ryker sunk his fingers into his dog's black fur. "Mom, what's wrong?"

Riley pieced together what she knew now of Lars's last night. He'd been here and lost his wallet somewhere in the snow, where Bear had found it. The dog had black hair.

"What time was that, Ryker?" Riley interjected softly. "When you chased Lars off the property?"

"Not sure, exactly. But I know it was after one. One thirty?"

And Lars had been in the back of Gloria's at one. "Did you get a good look at Lars that night? Did he have a jacket?"

"I thought it was strange that he wasn't wearing a coat," Ryker said. "But he was staggering drunk so I figured he'd lost it somewhere. Someone had popped him in the nose pretty good. There was blood all over his face."

So, after Coby had caught him in the safe. He would have

cash. Riley opened the wallet the dog had found. A thousand bucks. Where were his clothes? Lars had to have had something.

"No jacket, you say?"

"No. A black long-sleeved shirt."

Emily cried harder into her hands.

Lindsay stayed stuck to the wall as if she were Velcroed to it.

This family would need some serious healing to make it through this rift. She could see the love they had for one another...but would it be enough to overcome betrayal?

If Ryker was telling the truth...he might have been one of the last people to see Lars alive.

"Where did you find the wallet?"

He crossed his arms defensively. "Bear found it, not me."

"Where?"

Riley expected to hear him say by Emily's window, but was shocked when Ryker said, "By Mom's car. I thought it was her glove or something."

Sam's demeanor grew chilly.

Riley turned to the trembling woman against the wall. "Did you give Lars Sorenson a ride anywhere, Lindsay?"

Her lower lip quivered. "No. Of course not."

"Maybe he was breaking in," Ryker suggested. "We should check to see if anything is broken or missing!"

Riley thought that a sound plan. "Lindsay, where were you the night in question?"

"Home. With my family."

Nodding, Riley turned to Sam. "And you?"

"Why are you asking this?" Sam placed his hands on the table. "We can't possibly be under suspicion..."

"Just answer the question, sir."

Sam clenched his jaw. "We were all home that night watching movies like we do every Friday night."

"You saw each other all night?"

"Lindsay and I got into a fight, and I slept on the couch." Sam bristled with hurt and anger.

Emily's bombshell about being pregnant was not the main bombshell, unfortunately for the Hamilton family.

"What did you fight about? Me?" Emily cried softly. "I'm sorry I disappointed you."

"No, love, not about you." Sam gestured at his wife. "If you don't tell them I will."

Lindsay looked down at her hands.

Sam expelled a rush of air. "Your mother was having an affair with Lars."

Hurt and shock passed over Emily's face, and Ryker gasped in disbelief.

"Mom. I—I don't understand," Emily said. "How could you?"

Lindsay rushed to Emily's side. "Honey, I'm sorry. I didn't know. I didn't want anyone to find out. I never wanted to hurt you."

Emily got to her feet and pushed her away. Ryker pulled his sister by the arm and brought her to where he stood by the sink. United. Bear was at their feet. The pup had curly black hair. Different than what had been in Lars's hand.

Riley stepped back from the broken family, hoping they'd find their way. "I'm very sorry for your troubles. Emily, call me if you'd like my help with welfare assistance. I'd like you all to stay put as we continue our investigation."

"You think one of us killed Lars?" Lindsay said, aghast.

"I don't think anything." Riley had no respect for this woman, but it was her job not to judge. She kept her tone and demeanor polite. "I'm uncovering clues until I find out who did. I *will* find the murderer."

Sam raked his hand through his dark hair, sorrow in his eyes. "I hated him, but I wouldn't have killed him. Lindsay and I were going to try to stick it out for the kids, but that's changed now." He slumped, defeated.

It was probably for the best that the entire family get counseling. She'd talk to Rosita about it later.

Right and wrong she understood and believed in with all her heart. So how could she feel a tiny bit sorry for them all? Lars was poison and had destroyed their lives.

As she left the house, the family was quiet.

Riley walked around Lindsay's truck. No windows were broken, and any prints in the snow had been long covered. Toughen up, Harper, she told herself as she got in the SUV and started the engine. Who's to say that Lindsay or Sam didn't go after Lars that night? Lindsay, to meet her lover. Sam, to kill him.

CHAPTER SIXTEEN

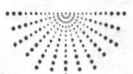

RILEY DROVE BY MURPHY'S MARINA, TEMPTED TO STOP IN AND chat with Bernie. He wasn't outside, but she pulled into the parking lot and watched the few boats in the water. Most had been put in storage, though these sturdy vessels seemed to have survived the winds. Could Lars have tried to steal the missing boat from the marina? Or had his killer been so desperate to leave the island that they'd braved the weather on a stolen dingy?

A thousand bucks had been left in the wallet. Money wasn't the motive for killing Lars, who'd had a bloody nose. Somewhere between Coby's and the Hamilton's, he'd been punched in the face.

By who?

Not Sam. Not Lindsay. Not Ryker. Not Coby.

Riley called Matthew, then cursed beneath her breath. "No cell service." She pressed the button for the radio.

"Sniders here."

"Matthew, it's Riley." Her adrenaline was in overdrive at all she'd just learned. Watching the bob of the boats on the bay was peaceful. A seagull caught a gust of wind, flying free.

"Sorry I couldn't make it, but as soon as I'd changed my tire, no easy task in this weather, guess who showed up on skis?" He didn't wait for her to guess but said, "Kimber and Tamara."

"What did they say?"

"Kimber confirmed everything that Coby told us. She was scared she might get in trouble for hitting Lars so hard—and then when she heard Lars was dead, she worried that she'd look guilty. I took her statement, and they just left. How'd your interview go?"

She gave him the rundown of what had happened at the Hamiltons. "I feel so bad for the family. I had hopes that the pup's fur might be a match, but Bear's got curly, not straight."

"I'll write the information you just gave me on our board."

Riley spoke her thoughts aloud as they occurred. "Be sure to add Tessa Barton's dog to the list—little Muffin has black fur too." She sighed, unable to get the image of Lars's bloody nose out of her mind. "Matthew, why didn't Lars go to Tessa's? She cared for him and it was likely that she'd have taken him in. Who did he get into a fight with?" She was sure that Tessa would have helped. "I'm going to Tessa's and get another look at that dog."

"That's a good idea."

She thought so too and checked the front of the marina's shop entrance one more time for Bernie, but he wasn't there. Riley had a better trail to follow so she left for the main road. "Have you heard from the chief?"

"He's chomping at the bit to get here, but there's nothing he can do."

"I'll be in touch."

Riley followed the plowed main road. The landscape was different layered in snow. The drifts on the side of the road showed that Crash, or some of the folks with plows, had cleared the streets. She realized that Tessa's was very close to Coby's and turned in the direction of The Shack instead.

Where did Lars go after he left Coby's? They'd found his broken phone and cigarette butt behind Katie and Carter's home. Had he stopped anywhere else in his midnight flight?

She drove to his place and parked. The street and parking lot of The Shack, right next door to his house, had been cleared by a plow and snowblower though a CLOSED sign hung on the door. Riley got out and surveyed his property, but she couldn't walk through it since the snow came to her waist. His backyard didn't have a fence, and it connected to an alley.

Two blocks over was Tessa's house. It made sense that Lars would run to where he knew he was wanted. He'd been told not to go the bar, not even as a customer. Lars owed Tessa money, but he could have offered to pay her with the cash he'd stolen from Coby.

She couldn't forget that Tessa's Muffin was a black dog and a strand of black fur had been in Lars's palm.

Riley recalled how protective Ethan had been of Tessa. He'd had on an oven mitt for the coffee pot. Her breath plumed before her as she hurried back to the SUV and climbed inside, driving toward Tessa's boarding house.

She arrived and used her boots to forge a path through two feet of snow which hadn't been shoveled yet today. Once on the porch, she scanned the pristine white patches with no fences. The Lobster Pot was less than a mile away.

Tessa answered the door with a smile. "Officer Harper! How are you?"

"Good. I take it you weathered the storm all right?"

"Oh, yes. Ethan and I have played one round of scrabble after another." Her pup sniffed Riley's ankles. Muffin's hair was short and wiry. Not like the hair Lars had in his hand. *Darn it.*

"May I come in? I have a few questions about Lars."

"Of course."

Riley followed her to the living room, where Ethan was

sipping something hot before the fireplace. He didn't quite meet her eyes—trying for too casual.

"Take a seat."

"Thanks." Riley chose an armchair and Tessa took the couch near Ethan. A game table was between them with the board on top. "You may have heard that Lars is dead?"

Tessa winced. "I did. I can't believe it. How?"

Riley shrugged. "We are still investigating." She deliberately and purposefully looked at Ethan's knuckles. Ethan's were yellowish in color. A few days ago, they'd probably been darker. Purple even. "It seems he was in a fistfight the night he disappeared, well, early in the morning."

"He was?" Tessa's hand came to her throat. "Oh, poor Lars."

Ethan's jaw tightened.

"Did you see Lars Sorenson that night?" Riley asked Tessa. "I'm sure he was coming your way."

"No! Of course not." Tessa shook her head with confusion in her troubled eyes.

Riley shifted to zero in on Ethan. "And you, Ethan? Did you see Lars? Maybe stop him from entering, with your fist?"

Tessa whirled toward her boarder, who glanced at his knuckles. Guilt emanated from him. "Ethan? You said you hit your hand against the door."

Ethan lifted his gaze to Tessa's. "I didn't want to tell you. God, you would have let Lars in again, even though he screwed you over. I was just trying to help."

Tessa grabbed Ethan's injured hand and studied it, then lifted her face to search Ethan's. "By beating him?"

"What happened, Ethan?" Riley asked, drawing their attention.

He cleared his throat and sipped from his mug. "I was watching the snow from my window and saw Lars enter the yard. I was alarmed until I realized who it was, and then I was just furious. I went downstairs and out the back before he could wake you."

"I can't believe this," Tessa said in shock. She released his hand.

Riley nodded at him. "What happened between you?"

"He pulled his wallet out of his jacket pocket, saying he needed to move back in. He had the money to pay you back. He didn't care that he hurt you—you were a means to an end. He said he could screw *you* and screw you over all he wanted—it was none of my business. He was right, so I punched him. It felt good so I did it again."

Tessa's mouth opened slightly. "And then?"

"I had him by the jacket as he tried to run away, loser, but I let him go and told him not to come back. I love you, Tessa. Can't you see that?"

Tessa sat back, her palm to her heart. "I had no idea. Ethan!"

"What time was that?" Riley asked.

"I don't know for sure. It wasn't one yet, I know that."

Riley stood. At midnight, Lars stole from Coby. He'd come to Tessa's, where Ethan had punched him. At one, he was seen by Matthew's neighbor. This fit for what Ryker had said about it being one thirty. Lars must have ran for the Lobster Pot, and panicked when Shep started barking—maybe he'd accidentally dropped the phone, and tried for Tessa's next. "Ethan, what happened to the coat? Do you have it?"

"No." Ethan pulled his gaze from Tessa. "But it was slipping off as he ran toward Main Street."

He brushed his hands together. Tessa grabbed one and kissed the top. "Thank you, Ethan. I had no idea."

That explained the bruises...and why Lars had wanted money. What had happened to Lars's clothes?

"I'll need you to come to the station and fill out a statement. Did you kill Lars Sorenson, Ethan?"

"No! God, no." He lifted his earnest face to Riley, without guile. "I'll come right now, if you want."

She went with her intuition and said, "Tomorrow is fine."

"Thank you, Officer," Tessa said as Ethan nodded.

"I'll let myself out." The two were staring at each other as if a veil had just been lifted. Riley hoped they'd be happy.

She passed through the foyer to the front door, escorted by Muffin who gave another little tail wag. Dogs offered companionship and unconditional love for their owners, no matter their owners' foibles.

Back in the SUV once more, Riley noticed a missed call from Kyra. This was great news, since it meant that she had cell phone service. A text came through.

When can we go home, Mom?

Riley immediately called her daughter, hoping nothing was wrong. "Hey, hon, what's up?"

"I finished my book and it feels weird to be in someone else's house. Can we go back to our place?"

"Sure! Is your nana ready?"

"Yep."

"I can be there in ten minutes, all right?"

"Thanks, Mom."

Riley switched most of her brain to Mom mode but kept a portion open to solving the problem of who had killed Lars. It worked that way sometimes when looking at an issue really hard, to step back and let the subconscious have a chance to figure it out while the rest of her was dealing with other also important things, like family.

"On my way!"

She tried to call Matthew again, but the call dropped on the third ring. It was progress that Riley didn't even get upset about it.

Reaching for the radio, she reached him right away. "Hey, partner. Just left Tessa's. Ethan is the one who popped Lars in the face. Lars was going to weasel his way into Tessa's good graces with the money he stole from Coby."

"Is Ethan our killer?"

"I don't believe so, but he'll be in tomorrow to give us a statement of his version of what happened. We have more for our timeline anyway. Listen, I'm headed to your parents' to pick up Mom and Kyra."

"Okay. Ma had so much fun, even with the storm. She misses having kids in the house. Why don't you come to the station after that? I have some things on the board that might interest you."

That was intriguing. "You got it!"

Riley drove to the Sniders' house. The main roads had been plowed but the side roads were still thick with snow. Some neighborhoods hadn't fared as well as the Sniders' or Tessa's, and she noticed portions of roof missing and lots of blue tarp covering it. Trees were bent in half, and power lines down. She saw a truck from Island Power and two men in rubber boots and orange jackets doing their best while it was still daylight.

Mostly she was impressed by how resilient the folks on Sandpiper Bay were in the aftermath of the storm.

She arrived at Matthew's parents' and parked in the driveway.

Alf was out front with the snowblower, though all of the neighbor's sidewalks were clear. Martha was also outside, chatting with Susan and Kyra, all in warm clothes, as if the sky was raining sunshine instead of gray and cloudy.

Riley parked in the drive and turned off the engine. Kyra grinned with relief to see her and hurried toward the SUV.

She got out and Kyra hugged her as if they'd been apart for years. "Mom!"

Susan lifted her hand in a wave but finished her conversation.

"Hey, Kyra." Riley searched her daughter's face for signs of anything wrong but noticed nothing obvious. She walked them toward Martha and Susan. "Wow, this looks terrific. You guys really cleaned the place up. Hard to tell there was even damage on this block."

"Everybody pitches in," Martha said. "Kyra and Susan kept the hot coffee and hot chocolate going. It felt like a block party."

Kyra's eyes pleaded with Riley to hurry up and get them out of there, and home. She side-hugged her daughter, then thanked everyone again, as did Susan and Kyra.

Riley put their luggage into the hatch, and they all piled in. Her mom buckled up in the passenger seat, and Kyra was in back. She kept smiling and waving to the Sniders, while waiting for her daughter to spill what was going on.

The tires spun as she gently stepped on the gas, in reverse, to the street. Once there, she put the gear in drive and her foot to the pedal. The tires whirred in place. She lifted her foot rather than step down harder and tried again. The SUV rocked forward and the traction of four-wheel drive caught.

Riley smiled at her mom, then Kyra through the rearview mirror. Her daughter wore a teenage pout.

"What's going on, hon? I know you had more than one book with you."

"I don't want to talk about it." Kyra stared out the window.

Riley looked at Susan. Her mom gave a little head shake. Not now, she conveyed. Riley nodded.

"What did you think of Martha, Mom?"

"I had a great time. She invited me to be part of their book club." Her mom tucked a gray strand of hair behind her ear, sounding chipper and upbeat.

"I'm so glad. I'm a little worried about the amount of clean up to be done at our house. I'm afraid that because of the case, I can't stay and help you."

Susan waved her hand. "We know you have to work, Riley. We are ready to tackle what we need to do, right, Kyra?"

Kyra mumbled an agreement.

Riley kept her attention on the slippery road. At last, she reached the main road, which had been plowed—but even that was slick. "Just prioritize the important stuff, like the fridge and fire. I'll make sure the generator is on. Some neighborhoods have hardly any damage, while others are covering holes in their roofs with blue tarps. Crazy. I hope I'll be able to get us to our front door."

"We don't mind walking," Susan said. "Do we, Kyra?"

"No." Kyra put in her earbuds, blocking out conversation.

What the heck had happened this morning? If her daughter was this moody, it usually had to do with missing her best friend, Sammy.

They passed the ferry depot and the chicken man's house, then arrived at their home. Snow decorated the roof like a painting of a winter wonderland, the white around the property undisturbed by footprints.

Riley made sure the SUV was in four-wheel drive, then teetered on the top of the dirt path leading down. She said a quick prayer and hovered her foot over the brake as she began her descent.

"Mom! Be careful!" Kyra's voice pitched high.

"You've got this," Susan said, even as she gripped the passenger door.

Thank God it wasn't steep was all she could think. She maneuvered them to the door with only a few half slides.

She blew out a breath and turned off the car. "Can you imagine if we'd had the Fiat?"

"It wouldn't have handled the snow as well," her mom said diplomatically.

"Or at all," Kyra countered.

Riley was the first out and she waded a path to the door. It was technically the entrance of the house, but they considered the view of the bay the front.

She went in and flicked on the light. Nothing. The power was off, but Don had showed her how to operate the generator, hopefully she remembered. God, had that only been two days ago?

Riley ducked into the attached garage and grabbed a snow shovel to clear a path for her mom. Kyra was already lugging their bags inside, along with the snow.

"It's cold in here," she said, sounding like she was ten instead of fourteen.

"I'm going to start up the generator, all right? You help Nana please."

Her daughter was on the verge of arguing, she could see, but logic saved the day as Kyra realized there was a lot to do, and she could help.

Kyra straightened her shoulders, then nodded. "'Kay."

"Oh dear," Susan said when she walked in. "I wonder how long the power has been out." Her mom beelined from the hallway to the kitchen where she opened the freezer. "It's still cold. I bet we haven't lost anything." Riley heard the fridge door next, then, "Even the milk is good."

Riley went to the large picture window and looked out. They'd lost two trees, both spindly pines, but in the lawn and not against the house. Matthew had assured her that they had enough firewood to see the winter out.

Kyra prepared the fireplace for a fire, still not in a talkative mood.

Riley hurried outside and shoveled a path from the front door to around the side of the house and the generator. Brushing the snow off the top, she started the machine. It rumbled to life and within seconds, the interior lights visible from the side window flickered on.

Thank you, Don, she thought. Helpless no more.

She went inside where Kyra sat before the fireplace, feeding small sticks of kindling to the blaze.

"Are you ready to tell me what happened today?" Riley rubbed her daughter's back.

Kyra's nose scrunched but then she nodded and glanced up at Riley. The best friends necklace was in her palm rather than around her neck. "Sammy and Josh kissed. Like, they're official now. He doesn't want her talking to me all the time."

"Oh, sweetheart. I'm sorry. Boyfriends come and go, but your girlfriends stick around."

"I don't have any friends."

She passed her hand down Kyra's long hair. "Maybe it's time to change that. Making new friends doesn't mean that Sammy's not your closest."

"It's not that easy."

"I know. I understand. You tell me how I can help, and I will."

Kyra gave another slow nod. "I'll think about it. There's this one girl in English, and she likes to read the classics too."

Riley kissed Kyra's head and stood. "Invite her over, if you want."

"Slow down, Mom! I don't need you to arrange my playdates anymore." Her lips twitched as she tried not to giggle.

"Backing off!"

She joined her mom in the kitchen and they talked about what had happened.

"It's a hard lesson," Susan said. "Time doesn't stand still and people move on. It's a good thing, in a way, for Kyra to learn that now, so that she can make new friends. Wherever we are. Now, don't you have a killer to find? We're okay. You go take care of the other folks who need you in Sandpiper Bay."

"You're the best, Mom."

The sky outside the picture window grew dark as if the storm would continue. Riley knew she had to hustle back to the station. The problem-solving part of her brain insisted that the dog hair and the king of spades mattered.

But how?

CHAPTER SEVENTEEN

It took several tries before Riley made it out of her driveway. This morning, Alf had used rock salt to tame the snow. She didn't have that, but she had plenty of gravel. Riley dug it free and put it behind the tires and voila! It worked.

Feeling victorious, she stepped a little too exuberantly on the gas pedal and the SUV slid. "Oops!" She lifted her foot and tightened her grip on the wheel. "Sorry."

She arrived at the station with perspiration on her brow and parked in the back next to Matthew's sedan. Susan had forced a peanut butter sandwich on Riley before she left, and it had been a much-needed boost of energy.

Entering the breakroom, Riley was glad to see Matthew surrounded by empty cracker packets and a half-eaten log of salami.

"Someone left us this gift of Hickory Farms for Christmas. It's a lifesaver since I already ate the last frozen pizza," he said with a laugh. "Help yourself."

Riley snagged a cracker and popped it in her mouth, taking off her coat and slinging it over the chair. She had no intention of going to her office when the board was right here. "What did you find?"

"I've added the spades playing card and the dog hair," Matthew said, sitting back. "And crossed Kimber from our suspect list."

Riley nodded, then stepped toward the board to pick up the marker. "I think we can eliminate the Hamiltons too, if we go by the dog hair."

She wrote a line through their name with satisfaction.

"And Tessa Barton. Her dog is a wire-haired terrier."

"Mark it off," Matthew agreed.

"And Coby." She tapped her chin with the capped pen.

She stared at the clues and the names. Miguel, from the liquor store. "Miguel was also in a fistfight. Nelson Bach."

"Who else played cards?"

Riley's scalp tingled—this was the right thread to follow. She hated to do it but added Trevor Dunfield. Crash Moreno. Charlie Higgins.

"Nelson told me about Lars having a tell—he touched the spades tattoo on his knuckle when he had a winning hand, and Nelson figured it out. Lars never won against Nelson after that."

Riley ran back over the conversations she'd had with both Nelson and Miguel. She crossed her arms and glared at the board.

"What?" Matthew asked, standing up to join her.

"Something doesn't track. Nelson said that he was the only one that Lars couldn't con. Yet Miguel clearly said that Lars owed him money, which meant that Lars had lost the poker game to Miguel but didn't pay. Who is telling the truth?"

Her skin rose with goose bumps.

Matthew grinned and circled Nelson's name. "He claims to be the best of the players. I think we need to have a conversation with the king of their poker group."

Riley got into her coat in triple time. "Yeah. You drive—I

might land us in a ditch or something." Speed was more important than ego on a case.

"Maybe we should try calling first," he suggested as they
darted out the back of the station, locking up, and getting into
Matthew's car. "To make sure he's home."

"Where else would he be?" Snow was beginning to fall and
that tingling feeling of alarm filled Riley. She glared at the thick
flakes hitting the glass. "Stop that, now..."

Matthew chuckled and put on the wipers, backing out of the
lot to the main road. It hadn't snowed all day until now which
meant that the roads were still clear.

She sat back with disappointment as a sour realization
reached her. "Only problem is that Nelson doesn't have a dog."

"That you know of," Matthew said. His tone was disappointed.

Riley still wanted to interview Nelson. "Does Miguel have a
dog? We know Crash does, but Shazam is brown. And Charlie?"

Matthew followed Park Road past Mackabee Woods, the
road to the Hamiltons, and the marina. Dogs of all sizes raced
around the front entrance.

"The dog hair isn't a viable clue," she said. "Not like the card.
The king of spades. Nelson considered himself the best player
of them all. Why would someone cram it in Lars's throat?"

"It's true that everybody and their brother has a dog or a cat.
I thought it was good, though, Riley. We'll keep it on the back
burner."

Matthew was a much better and supportive partner than her
last one had been. That hadn't ended well. She knew that if put
in the same position, Matthew wouldn't have fired his weapon
at the unarmed man.

Though young, he had integrity that was surprisingly rare.

He slowed as they passed an area beside the road that was
pristine snow. Trees had protected the area somewhat and there
was only five feet max accumulated around the shanties.

"My grandpa used to have his shack right there. He'd make a big fire pit in the back next to a hole in the ground where he'd fish. You had to go real deep he taught me, because the fish go toward the bottom of the ocean to stay warm. It's not as deep here in the bay so there was good fishing."

"It's been plowed through here," Riley noted.

"Crash probably did it for his buddies. He's got a shanty too, Charlie said."

Smoke curled from two of the shacks—one of them being Nelson's. They parked, and he answered at the first knock. Shazam got up from the floor with a woof in greeting.

"Some watch dog you'd make, bud." Nelson patted Shazam on the head. "Lay down now."

Riley and Matthew exchanged a look. Maybe Nelson was the king linchpin after all.

"Hello, Nelson." Riley adjusted her stance casually, making sure she had access to both her taser and her gun.

"Nelson! Can we come in?" Matthew asked.

"Sure, sure. Nobody breathe out or we might knock the place over, but yeah." Nelson ushered them toward his table for two. "Mi casa and all that."

Matthew entered but Riley held back to block the front door. Casually. "That's Shazam, right?"

"Yep," Nelson confirmed. "I'm dog sitting. You here because of the Fiat?"

"No. What's wrong with it? I need to pick it up as soon as it's ready." She couldn't borrow the chief's beyond Tuesday morning, when he came home.

"Well, the storm knocked down a lot of trees, as you probably noticed." Nelson sipped his cup of gin, then set it on the counter.

"Yes, we have. Was the auto shop affected? Roof down?"

"No. Just the Fiat." He snuck another fast drink. "It's insured, ain't it?"

She stilled. "Tell me."

"It was smashed by a tree. Clean down the middle, the owner said."

Riley couldn't process the unwelcome news. A small car was better than no car. But half a car? Not fair!

Shazam wagged his tail sadly and black-brown fur colored the tile. Straight fur. Riley studied the big dog that was a mix of everything—mostly brown, but there was black too.

Her body went on high alert. "Nelson, I'd like for you to be very honest about the questions I'm going to ask. Did you see Lars Sorenson Friday night or Saturday?"

His cheeks flushed and he glanced at a card on the counter next to a deck. The king of spades was face up. A bottle of gin was about half filled. A cup was full. No ice.

"I didn't see him, no."

"Can you explain that card to me?" She'd seen one at Miguel's too. It matched the one in Lars's throat.

"I found it under my door when I came home on Friday. Didn't comprehend at first but then I talked to Crash, Charlie, and Miguel. Everybody in our group got one."

"Who gave it to you? Lars?" Riley wondered if that was what Lars had been doing after getting off the ferry Friday morning. Threatening his old poker buddies. Why?

"I had Charlie Google it." Nelson winced. "It's supposed to mean *death*."

"Why would Lars do that to all four of you?" Riley nodded at the card. "I'd like it for evidence."

"Never said it was Lars." Nelson backed up and accidentally stepped on Shazam. The dog whined. "Sorry, bud. He got into something in the woods and hurt his paw. Crash put salve on it and had Trevor look at it. It's a pretty deep cut."

Riley pulled out gloves and a plastic bag she kept in her pocket, carefully putting the card into the bag. "Don't play games with me, Nelson. Did Lars threaten you?"

Nelson's chin quaked. "Could be."

"Why would he?" Matthew asked. "You played cards together. You're pals."

Nelson whirled toward Matthew. "No, we aren't. Lars was a damn cheater, that's why. We kicked him off the island and told him to never come back."

"You, Crash, Miguel, and Charlie threatened Lars almost five months ago to the point he *left* the island?" Riley asked in disbelief. "Voluntarily?"

"Mostly. He's a cheater and can't be trusted." Nelson drew up self-righteously. "Heard he knocked up that innocent Emily Hamilton."

"How on earth did you hear that already?" Riley asked.

"Down at the marina...I snowshoed up the hill to see how folks were and it was all anybody was talking about. I bet that Sam Hamilton, if he wants to keep his family together, will sell and move away to start over."

Riley held up her hand. "Let's stay on track, Nelson. When was the last time you saw Lars Sorenson?"

"I know exactly. It was when we caught him cheating Miguel. He owed Miguel thousands and had no means to make the debt square. We had a meeting and decided that it was time for Lars to move on. We all have roots here and he don't belong. His family's long dead."

"How did you do it? I have a hard time believing he'd just go because you told him to," Riley said.

Nelson gulped. "Maybe, we used a weapon..."

"What kind?" Riley demanded.

"A gun." He reached for his gin and drank. "Me and Miguel took Lars across to Camden in Crash's tugboat by gun point. Told him to leave, and consider the debts squared unless he came back. He never shoulda come back."

This explained why Lars had stiffed Tessa and asked for his stuff to be sent. He hadn't intended on leaving Sandpiper Bay.

"Did you owe him money, any of you?"

"No. I told he, he was a damn cheater. He mighta won occasionally but not honestly."

Why come back? Riley looked at Matthew, who was taking notes with pen and paper. "It's possible that Lars returned for revenge. But then what? He handed out the King of Spades death cards. The storm trapped him on the island."

"And someone killed him first," Matthew said.

It fit. Riley nodded. "Where is Crash? I'd like to question him too." And then Miguel and Charlie. Especially Miguel.

"Crash had some errands to run. Don't know where—he didn't say. Just asked me to take care of Shazam. Why?"

Riley didn't answer but asked, "Did the games ever get physical in nature?"

"Lars was a sore loser." Nelson shrugged. "Got drunk and liked to fight."

"Who fought back, usually?"

Nelson's ears colored. "Crash."

The man had shoulders like a linebacker and muscles from working the tugboat. He had very large hands. Much larger than Miguel. "Let's go talk to him, Matthew. His cottage is by the woods." A tingle raced up her spine. Riley could put Crash by Mackabee, where Lars had been the night he'd tried to see Emily. After one thirty in the morning. The doctor had placed his time of death probably around two.

"Where is his shed?" Riley wanted to check that out.

Nelson's chin quivered. "On the other side, closest to the woods. But you can't reach it direct. It's snowed over. Best to take the other road."

"Let's go," Riley said to Matthew. Her nerves were singing that they had to move, and quick.

Matthew stood so fast the chair hit the wall. "You don't talk to a soul, Nelson."

"I won't." Nelson raised his palm, his body trembling. "Swear."

Riley and Matthew left the shanty and Matthew drove like the hounds of hell were after them. The slick snowy roads made it a harrowing journey. "Murder is a lot different than cheating at cards," she said. "Let's try his cabin first."

Four minutes later, Matthew brought the sedan to the front of Crash's place. Smoke drifted into the air, but not from the lone chimney stack.

"Behind the house!" Riley said, running to the back. There was no path shoveled, so she followed the trampled footsteps made by a man with large feet. She slipped and slid but managed to keep her forward momentum.

Matthew bumped into her when she stopped suddenly. There was a bare-bones deck attached to the property holding a shovel and tools. A long fishing knife. Crash's thick coat was slung on the wood and sweat poured down his face, despite the forty-degree weather. Black rubber boots reached his knees. His brown hair streaked with gray was wild and messy.

He kept tossing things into a fire with flames about four feet high in a circular stone fire pit. He'd cleared snow in a six by ten circle.

"Crash! What are you doing?"

The last of a leather jacket sleeve was going up in flames. Next, he fed in a black shirt. Riley noticed a scruffy duffle bag kicked over, with playing cards randomly strewn. Was that Lar's missing bag? Where had it been?

His expression when he saw them was pure fear, then resignation. He eyed the distance to the woods six feet away. It wouldn't be an easy jog as he'd have to break through four feet of snow about waist high.

"Stop what you're doing!" Riley ordered. "We've been to Nelson's. We saw Shazam, and we know that Lars threatened you."

Crash flinched and rubbed his knuckles, covered in thick winter gloves. Had he been wearing gloves the last time she'd seen him? He must've been. It was winter in Maine. Perfect camouflage for injuries on his hands.

He kicked in the duffle bag part of the way and Riley stopped herself from jumping toward it to save evidence. Instead, she patted the holster of her weapon. She had a gun, and a taser. "Don't move, Crash. Don't make things worse on yourself."

"It was an accident," Crash said, not meeting her eyes.

"Choking your poker partner was not an accident," Riley said coolly. Matthew staggered next to her at the blatant assessment but nodded.

This was a man he knew, that he'd grown up with. She kept her focus on Crash. In all her career, she'd never fired her weapon at someone, but it was part of her training—she could do it but would rather find another way. Keep him talking, she thought. "Did Lars cheat you too? We can help you, Crash."

Crash glanced toward the line of trees again. The snow was a four-foot barricade around them, except for the area he'd cleared for the fire pit. His answer was a grunt.

"Did he ask to stay with you? Call on your friendship?"

Crash's jaw clenched. "We weren't friends. I caught him putting the death card in my house."

Riley nodded encouragingly. "Breaking and entering is a crime."

Crash nudged the bag farther into the flames.

"What did he want?" Matthew asked. "Money? Revenge?"

Crash gulped and looked at Matthew, then back at the fire. "He wanted both. Told me he crossed the wrong people in Bangor, and owed them a lot more than he owed us. They tried to kill him, and he came here." He scrubbed his jaw with his gloved hand and met Riley's gaze, then Matthew's, searching for understanding. "Lars had nowhere else to go. Any injured animal will return to its den. He realized real quick nobody wanted him here. He figured he'd scare us as payback for making him leave, steal from us, and take the money to Canada to start over." Crash shook his head, eyes hard. "Idiot."

"You caught him in your house that morning, and you let him go?" Riley asked, confused. Her arms were at her sides, ready to act if he made a move.

"I was home for lunch." Crash knocked one big fist into an open palm. "The coward ran. Shazam chased him off the property. I warned him that if I saw him again, I'd kill him—not the other way around. He didn't have the balls to hurt anyone."

Riley tried to imagine what happened that night—a drunk and lost Lars racing around during a storm desperate to find shelter. "And he didn't listen?"

Crash punched his fist into his hand with a resounding smack. "Nope. He thought he could hide out in the shanties and try to flee the island, but he was trapped like a rat. Not the brightest. You don't threaten people who live here. This is my home. I won't be threatened in it."

That didn't sound like an accident, Riley thought. That was a decision made—maybe in anger, but a decision to kill.

"What happened, Crash?" Matthew asked softly.

"Lars picked up a fishing knife somewhere—they're all over the place. I've got them in mine." He nodded to the blade on his porch. "Shazam found his jacket, and we used it to track him to an empty fishing shed. He attacked me and Shazam got in the way. He hurt my dog. It was the last straw."

Crash looked out at the trees longingly. She sensed he was close to bolting even though it would be impossible to outrun them. "You searched for him, in the storm."

"He threatened me, and my friends." His voice was cold. "My dog."

"How?"

His nose flared. "You'll find a dog sled at my shanty. High-powered headlamp. Shazam's got a great sense of smell and he's always hated Lars."

This was premeditated murder. "Step away from the fire," Riley said. "Put your hands up."

Crash did as instructed. His broad shoulders strained his shirt.

Matthew slowly rounded the fire, his hand on his taser as he blocked the direct route toward the woods in the cleared area. "Your property and your animal were threatened."

"Lars was trash." Crash trembled. "Drunk. Stupid with it, you know? He blamed us for his bad luck when he'd brought it on himself." He slowly removed his glove. Riley could see that the fist was swollen and purple, probably broken.

"Did you plan this with Nelson and Miguel? Trevor?" Riley asked. Her mental game was clear—find out the facts of what happened, and then arrest him.

"No—no, it was just me. We weren't scared of him. At the end," Crash swallowed, "he begged for just enough to get to Canada and start over. It was too late." He glanced around the fire to the woods.

"He was already dead?" Matthew asked.

"Near enough. I shoved that damn card down his throat. I'd planned on dumping his body in the ocean but that damn Ryker was snooping around. I couldn't chance getting caught. I stuck Lars in the fishing shed to deal with later. I don't know how he ended up in the ditch—for me to uncover." He coughed as if in horror at what had happened. What he'd done.

Riley didn't share that Crash had only been caught because of a wild animal.

Crash lowered his arms slightly. "I don't deserve to go to jail for a piece of trash like Lars." He lobbed the rest of the duffel bag into the flames with his foot. Riley wanted that evidence, though this was a confession.

"Where did you get that bag?" she asked.

"In the shanty he was hiding in—next to mine, like I wouldn't find him? Desperate people make mistakes."

Riley saw the exact moment when Crash decided to compound his bad decisions. His body tensed and he raced right toward Matthew, pushing her partner down into the snow.

She leaped over the fire with super-human strength to save Matthew from being hurt and jammed the end of the taser against Crash's thick neck. The big man jolted with electricity, and she shoved him off of Matthew. Matthew scrambled to his feet with his gun drawn and pointed it at Crash.

Riley slid on the snow but gained traction and within seconds she had Crash's arms behind his back and handcuffed, her knee in his back. The big man sobbed, asking that Nelson look after Shazam.

"You're right, Crash. Desperate people do make mistakes—like you," Matthew said, hand steady as he holstered his gun.

"Crash Moreno," Riley said, her voice calm as her adrenaline soared. "I am placing you under arrest for the murder of Lars Sorenson."

EPILOGUE

TUESDAY AFTERNOON, RILEY AND HER PARTNER, MATTHEW, enjoyed a brief moment of recognition from their boss. Captain Bradley Barnes had arrived by ferry that morning, pleased with the news that Lars's killer, Crash Moreno, was locked up in their jail. Matthew was going to escort Crash to a larger facility with maximum security the next day. Nelson had agreed to keep Shazam.

Barnes raised his glass to all those seated around the lunch table. Rosita was chatting with Nancy, but everyone fell silent when Captain Barnes spoke.

He clinked glasses with Matthew, then Riley, his face flushed with pleasure.

"It's great to be back, I gotta tell you. Family's good, but all you here are family too."

Staggered by his words, Riley wondered what his glass contained.

The preferred champagne toast was substituted with fizzy ice drinks since they were in a police station, not a bar.

"I gotta say that I'm mighty pleased to see that these young officers managed the last week without me. Which kind of hurts too."

They all politely laughed, and Riley wondered what he'd say next.

"Matthew." He turned and shook the younger man's hand. "I'm proud of you, boy; you're one fine cop." The captain stepped back. "Nobody in their right mind would have thought our old friend Crash would be capable of such a thing. But you two smarty pants went through the list of possibilities, ticking them off one at a time."

He gestured to the whiteboard. The list of suspects, lines crossed over the innocent, clues and guesses and questions answered, showed step by step how they had narrowed it down and based their conclusion on facts. "Add here that Bernie said no boats were taken that night, and the one he'd had to report as stolen, was found against the rocks. We should be able to get a time stamp of when exactly Lars used his phone, but from what you've got here, I bet you're right."

Barnes turned to Riley. "Have to say, Riley, you surprised me." He swirled his glass of fizzy lemonade. "You weren't what I expected. My mistake. Sure I was hard on you, and you held firm, not taking my crap. Thought I could get rid of you, but you stuck around like a stick of gum." He chuckled. "This is the second murder that you and Matthew have solved on the island."

Rosita and Nancy clapped and cheered.

"Let's all raise our glasses in a toast to two fine cops, Matthew Sniders and Riley Harper, well done."

Barnes clinked their glasses and they all took a quick sip. Matthew grinned and gave Riley a hug. She felt a sting of happy tears but not one spilled over.

"Thank you, Captain Barnes. I'm glad I could be of service." She could feel her cheeks grow warm.

"So, what are you thinking? Still leaving after your contract is up?"

"That decision hasn't been made, Chief." She turned her gaze to Matthew, wondering if he knew where this turn of conversation was headed. He shook his head.

"I've been doing some heavy thinking over the past few days." Barnes slugged back the rest of his drink and smacked it on the table.

Riley held her breath and glanced around at all the blank expressions. She wasn't being ambushed. No one had a clue.

Rosita had wandered over to give Matthew a hug. He didn't see her coming. His half glass was raised as her arm swept around his shoulder. He jerked and the drink splashed over both of them.

Nancy had been cutting the large celebratory chocolate cake and halted, knife in the air as they all sputtered with laughter, watching Matt and Rosita mopping each other's shirts.

When they each had a small plate of cake and a refill of the pretend champagne, Rosita and Nancy took their seats again. Barnes leaned against a corner of the table, his feet crossed in a comfortable position.

His posture opposed the tick in his cheek, the moisture in his eyes.

Riley stepped over to him, ready to meet him face-to-face. "You mentioned your heavy thinking a minute ago. Is it something you'd like to share with me?"

"Yes and no. We've gotta get you a car now that the Fiat is split in half."

Matthew gave a hearty laugh and winked at her. "She always did hate that car."

Everyone seemed to think it was funny, except the Chief and her.

The others in the room watched closely. The tension was palpable.

"What kind of a car, sir?" Riley asked.

"Well, that all depends." He stuck his hands in his pocket.

"On what, Chief?"

"How long you might be staying."

"Seven more months. Arrived late August. Leave late August." She felt herself getting warm. Butterflies flitted around inside. "I would like an SUV for this winter if that is within your budget."

The three others in the room watched closely.

The chief didn't answer right away, so Riley spoke again. "Probably a rental or short lease would be best. Secondhand, unless of course you have a good officer coming in to take my place."

Suddenly the ladies began clearing the plates, and Matthew offered to help.

Barnes choked, his face a darker shade of red.

"You can't stop, can you?"

Riley was surprised when a slow smile crept over his face.

"I know my place, sir, and think I understand. This is a difficult position for a woman with a mother and teenaged daughter to accept—even for one single year."

"I would hate to see you go." He rubbed his jaw. "What do you want? Me to beg?"

"No! Certainly not. But I have my family to consider, and my daughter needs a good education."

"I get that. She should go to Portland, plenty of great schools."

"If you're asking me for a commitment, I can't. I will give you that decision closer to the time when our contract comes up."

Matthew stepped up. "That's only fair, Chief. They haven't been here long enough to know whether or not they can make this home."

Barnes sighed. "I know that. Unfortunately, I may have to

retire someday soon. But not today or tomorrow. We'll take it a day at a time."

"Thank you, Chief."

"As far as that car is concerned, one will be arriving tomorrow."

"Dare I hope it's better equipped than that poor unfortunate Fiat, who took one for the team?"

Matthew chuckled.

Barnes answered. "Yes. A nice, four door Hyundai SUV, only three years old, with thirty thousand miles on it."

"It won't rack up the mileage around here, that's for sure."

"Okay then. You get the car, and this conversation is on hold."

"Aye, aye, sir. And I can't wait to tell Kyra and my mom. They will be grateful as well." She beamed. "It sure will be hard to leave all this great lobster behind."

The end.

If you enjoyed this book, please pick up the first in the Riley Harper Mystery — Death in SandPiper Bay buy here!

ABOUT THE AUTHORS

AUTHOR BIO: PATRICE WILTON

NEW YORK TIMES, bestselling author, PATRICE WILTON knew from the age of twelve that she wanted to write books that would take the reader to faraway places. She was born in Vancouver, Canada, and had a great need to see the world that she had read about.

Patrice became a flight attendant for seventeen years and traveled the world. At the age of forty she sat down to write her first book—in longhand! Her interests include tennis, pickleball, traveling, and writing stories for women of all ages.

She is best known as a popular romance author with 35 heartwarming stories on her resume. She is especially proud of her bestselling contemporary romance series, Paradise Cove, Heavenly Christmas, and the Wounded Warriors. Co-writing with Traci Hall, they have assumed the name Traci Wilton for the Salem B&B mystery series published by Kensington.

AUTHOR BIO: TRACI HALL

From contemporary seaside romances to cozy mysteries, USA Today bestselling author Traci Hall writes stories that captivate her readers. As a hybrid author with over fifty published works, Ms. Hall has a favorite story for everyone.

Mystery lovers, be on the lookout for her Salem B&B Mystery series, co-written as Traci Wilton, and her Scottish

Shire series, which takes place in the seaside town of Nairn, as Traci Hall.

Whether it's her ever popular By the Sea series, the next Appletree Cove sweet romance, or a fun who-done-it, Traci finds her inspiration in sunny South Florida, by living right near the ocean.

Writing as Traci Hall, Scottish Shire mysteries
Murder in a Scottish Shire July 2020
Murder in a Scottish Garden May 2021
Murder at a Scottish Social 2022

Traci Hall also writes historical romance, western romance, teen paranormal, new adult paranormal, coming of age, and non-fiction books.

Go to: TraciHall.com to learn more

OTHER BOOKS BY TRACI HALL AND PATRICE WILTON--WRITTEN AS TRACI WILTON

Traci Wilton is a pseudonym of Traci Hall and Patrice Wilton. Patrice Wilton is the *New York Times* and *USA Today* bestselling author of more than thirty books, some indie-published and some published by Amazon/Montlake. Traci Hall is the USA Today bestselling hybrid author of more than 50 books from cozy mystery to romance. Visit them at traciwilton.com

- Mrs. Morris and the Ghost August 2019
- Mrs. Morris and the Witch 2020
- Mrs. Morris and the Ghost of Christmas Past September 2020
- Mrs. Morris and the Sorceress March 30, 2021
- Mrs. Morris and the Vampire August 2021
- Mrs. Morris and the Pot of Gold 2022

A Note from the Authors

Thank you for reading DANGER AT SANDPIPER BAY

If you enjoyed this book, I'd appreciate it if you'd help others find it so they can enjoy it too.

- Lend it: This e-book is lending-enabled, so feel free to share it with your friends.
- Recommend it: Please help other readers find this book by recommending it to friends, readers' groups, and discussion boards.
- Review it: Let other potential readers know what you liked or didn't like about.

If you'd like to sign up for TRACI WILTON'S newsletter to receive new release information, please visit www.traciwilton.com

THANK YOU